Fae and Felonies

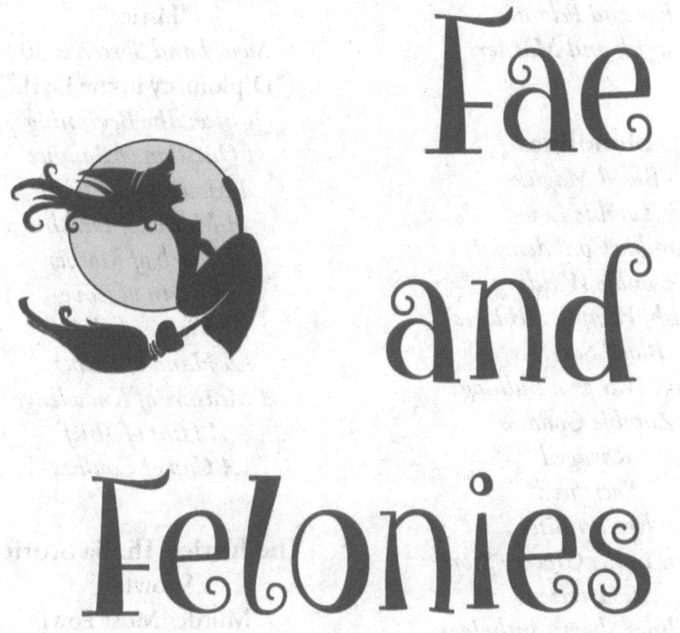

Suzan Harden

More Books by Suzan Harden
(Each series is in suggested reading order)

Millersburg Magick Mysteries
Spells and Sleuths
Fae and Felonies
Magick and Murder

Bloodlines
Blood Magick
Zombie Love
Zombie Confidential
Zombie Wedding
Amish, Vamps & Thieves
Blood Sacrifice
Love, War & a Bulldog
Zombie Goddess
Ravaged
Sacrificed
Reality Bites
Ghouls in the Grocery Store
Resurrected
Bloodlines Shorts Anthology
Bloodlines: The First Boxed Set

Seasons of Magick
Spring
Summer
Autumn
Winter
The Seasons of Magick Anthology

Justice
Sword and Sorceress 28
("Justice")
Sword and Sorceress 30
("Diplomacy in the Dark")
Justice: The Beginning
A Question of Balance
A Modicum of Truth
A Matter of Death
A Touch of Mother
A Twist of Love
A Virtue of Child
A Hand of Father
A Measure of Knowledge
A Hint of Thief
A Cup of Conflict

The Justice Thalia Stories
Snowfall
Murder Most Fowl
The Sweetest Poison
A Granddaughter of Mine
Too Many Fish in the Sea

Tales of the Twelve
The Trickster Priestess and the Demon

Crossover Worlds
Invasion!

888-555-HERO
Hero De Facto
Hero Ad Hoc
Hero De Novo
A Very Hero Christmas
Hero De Jure
Hero In Camera
Hero Amicus Curiae
A Very Hero Wedding
Hero Ad Litem
Queer Eye for the Super Guy

Solar System Services, Inc.
Alone Is Not Lonely
Halloween Harvest ("A Place at the Table")

Soccer Moms of the Apocalypse
Pestilence in Pumpkin Spice
Famine In French Vanilla
War in White Chocolate
Death in Double Mocha
Demons Run at Halloween

Miscellaneous
Sword and Sorceress 31 ("Pig-Headed")
Sword and Sorceress 32 ("Unexpected")
Practical Witches
Revenge Served Hot
The Yule Switch
Chocolate for Dinner
Silver Shoes and Pigs' Ears

For updates, news, and giveaways, join Suzan's mailing list or visit her website at www.suzanharden.com. You can also check her out on Facebook @SuzanHardenWriter.

This is a work of fiction. All characters, organizations and events in this story are products of the author's imagination and are not to be construed as real. Any resemblance to persons, living or dead, is entirely coincidental.

FAE AND FELONIES
(Millersburg Magick Mysteries #2)
Copyright © 2023 by Suzan Harden
All rights reserved.

ISBN-13 - 978-1-938745-78-2

Published by Angry Sheep Publishing
Findlay, Ohio

Interior Design by JW Manus
Cover Design by Valerie Lennox

To retired Dresden Police Chiefs

Kenneth "Kenny" Wolford

and

Jeff "Goober" Garver

Chapter 1

Kaley Wilson scribbled frantically on her trig worksheet. The white paper practically glowed underneath the energy efficient LED fixtures. The dang light didn't feel natural. The softer yellow ones would have been much more comfortable to both Normal and witch eyes, but West Holmes School District had to go with the lowest bidder.

What was the formula for a tangent again? She ignored classmates filtering into homeroom as she flipped through her notes, but she couldn't filter out their scents. Nothing like the odor of manure on boots to overpower the stink of dry-erase markers and ruin one's concentration.

She found the right page, scribbled down the correct formula, and started working through the next equation. How could she be an identical twin, yet advanced math was a breeze for Kirsten? And her sister refused to help her with homework last night.

Okay, maybe she shouldn't have been catching up on the post boys' basketball game gossip with Bella Sims until midnight before she asked Kirsten for assistance. Kaley realized she forgot to carry the one and scrubbed the mistake with her eraser. If only Principal Reed hadn't suspended her from cheerleading for the week for skipping study hall on Monday. But no, Reed still held a grudge over his attempt to suspend her for fighting when all she did was step out of the way of a blow fellow cheerleader Amelia Ryder aimed at her head in the girl's locker room, so he refused to overlook one little misstep.

If Mom and Dad hadn't grounded her, too, she could have snuck into the game, picked up some details about Brad and Amelia's breakup, flirted with Josh Fairbanks a bit, and gotten her homework done, instead of fretting in her bedroom the entire night about the whole situation. Kaley was pretty certain Josh was into her, but for all his exploits on the football field, he was shy when it came to the opposite gender. He just needed a little encouragement.

Crap! She used the formula for sine, not cosine. She flipped her pencil and erased the two lines she'd screwed up.

And who the heck needed trigonometry anyway? No one used it in fashion marketing.

As she tried to explain to Mom and Dad, who refused to listen.

Hope Stillwell nudged Kaley's arm with the eraser end of her pencil.

"Stop it!" Kaley hissed without looking up. "I'm trying to get this last problem—"

"Hottie at two o'clock."

Kaley looked up at the same moment alien magick tingled across her skin, raising the hairs on her arms and legs. A chill ran through her. She didn't need the feel of his power to know the boy who stood in the doorway and stared at her was fae. The white shock of hair wasn't a color you saw on most Normals, even with the help of modern dyes.

The fae was tall as most Unseelie were. His platinum hair made his tanned skin stick out and accented his brilliant blue eyes. He actually wore jeans and a sweatshirt under his coat, instead of glamouring Normal clothing. When she stared back, he quickly dropped his gaze and stalked to the back of the room. So, he knew what she was, too.

Worry gripped her, and she automatically solidified her mental and magickal shields. The last thing they needed was even an incidental interaction between their energies. The mix wasn't like oil and water. It was more like matter and anti-matter. And such an interaction usually resulted in the death of both the witch and the fae in question. In this close of quarters, they could take out their teacher and the entire class, too.

After the Battle of Millersburg, why the hell would the Winter Queen break the truce by sending one of her people to Holmes County?

Kaley resisted the urge to turn around and look at him again. The fae aged at a much slower rate than humans, even those with longer lifespans like witches and weres, so he could be older than her great-aunt Jo. The only people comparable to the fae were the vampires, and the fae viewed them as diseased cheaters because their extended life was courtesy of the V-virus.

"Why would someone change schools this late in the year?" Hope whispered.

"The middle of November isn't that late in the school year," Kaley whispered back. "And he may not have had a choice." Which was true if he was under orders from the Winter Queen.

Kaley turned back to the problem, but her concentration was totally destroyed. The bell rang, and Mrs. Thomas started calling roll. She'd have to take the hit on her homework score.

But that didn't bother her as much as the fae sitting behind her.

Kaley spotted her identical twin sister in the cafeteria. Well, identical if Kaley didn't dye her hair blond. Kirsten kept the rich mahogany color they'd been born with, the same shade as Mom and Aunt Jo's hair.

Kirsten sat with Hope and the rest of the varsity girls basketball team. Kaley charged over to their table and plopped down across from her sister. "I need to tell you something—"

"I'm not doing your damn homework." Kirsten glared at her as she shoved a forkful of green beans into her mouth.

"No," Kaley snapped. "There's a new boy—"

"Crap!" Hope grinned. "I forgot to tell you about the hot new guy who showed up in trig class this morning."

"Tall and cute in an emo way," Olivia Burke added in a dreamy voice. Her reaction didn't make sense. She didn't swing toward boys.

Kirsten looked at Olivia, frowned, and looked back at Kaley. *What's going on?* she asked telepathically.

He's fae.

"You're kidding, right?" Kirsten said aloud. Her brown eyes widened, and worry flowed past her mental shields. Kaley was fairly certain her sister's expression was the same one she had on her face before the morning bell.

"Not about this," she said. *I texted Mom and Jo between classes, but I haven't gotten an answer yet.*

"Why would anyone want to move here this late in the school year?" Kirsten said.

Hope made a face. "That's what I said."

Kirsten ignored her friend. "You think he's related to the guys who messed with the Amish years ago?"

Kaley shrugged. "Because of the murders, the corridor project stalled. They did invest a ton of money into the properties that would have adjoined the exit ramps and paid to get them rezoned for commercial use."

"What the heck are you guys talking about?" Olivia looked at Kaley and Kirsten like they spoke in a foreign language.

"Some ancient family history—" Kirsten's expression changed from contemplative to solemn. "The principal is walking this way. Behave yourself."

Kaley resisted the urge to roll her eyes. She looked over her shoulder as his shadow fell across her.

"Good afternoon, ladies." Principal Reed's voice was genial, but the emotion never reached his eyes. "Kirsten, we have a new student River Martin who started today. I need you to meet with him after school. Help him get caught up."

She cocked her head. "You do realize I have basketball practice?"

"Practice doesn't start until three-thirty, which is forty-five minutes after school ends." His tone didn't leave any room for Kirsten to argue.

She plastered on a fake smile. "All right. Tell him to meet me in the library. But it'll have to be thirty-five minutes so I have a chance to change and warm up."

"Fine," Principal Reed said.

Kaley watched him stroll toward Amelia Ryder who was sitting at a nearby table with half of the cheerleading squad. Well, technically, Amelia was sitting in her decorated wheel chair.

"He could have at least said 'please' and 'thank you,'" Kirsten grumbled under her breath while the principal attempted to flirt with the cheerleaders. His whole act made Kaley sick to her stomach. Good grief, the man was old enough to be the girls' grandfather. She turned back to Kirsten and the rest of the basketball team.

Hope shook her head. "That would mean acknowledging students as real people."

"Still, this is our chance to check out the new kid," Kaley said.

Kirsten's jaw worked before she said, "Think you can get Donny to come with us when we meet this new guy?"

Kaley considered her words. Kirsten was totally oblivious to Donny Fryer's crush on her. Donny threatened to bite Kaley if she said anything. Yet, her sister kept asking for his help with supernatural matters though she claimed he was trouble like the remaining werecoyotes in Holmes County.

"I can ask him," Kaley said. "But why?"

Kirsten scowled. "If we can't defend ourselves, Donny can rip the new kid's throat out."

Chapter 2

After the last class of the day, Kirsten leaned against the wall outside of the library. The off-white-painted plasterboard cooled the nervous perspiration that dampened the back of her blue Knights t-shirt. She'd never met a fae before, and the family stories about them had not been complimentary.

Especially not after the Winter Queen's assassin had orchestrated the murders of several Normals in Holmes County in his effort to trap and kill a newborn goddess. The great-grandfather of Mary Levy, one of her closest friends, had been a victim of the fae assassin's plot. Last month, Kirsten's former 4-H advisor Rose Gleason feared her brother, another victim, haunted her house. Thankfully, that wasn't the case.

Donny Fryer strolled up to Kirsten, his red backpack slung over his shoulder. An old Carhartt hooded tan jacket covered his navy t-shirt and well-worn jeans. He was a couple inches shorter than her five-eight, but he carried himself like a much bigger guy. Any Normal bullies who tried to harass him in elementary school had learned the hard way not to mess with him. Even the other werecoyotes in the county had started giving him a wide berth over the last year. Donny wasn't someone who backed down from a fight.

"Kaley said you needed my help." He smirked.

The last thing Kirsten wanted was to admit such a need, especially to Donny. But facing the fae boy alone didn't seem like such a great idea.

"Did she tell you why?"

He shrugged. "Something about protection from the new kid who started here today. Like you really need protection from anyone."

"She didn't tell you?" Kirsten wanted to track down her sister and kick her ass. This wasn't something she could spring on Donny. Not after what happened to his dad before Donny was born.

A muttered "Ah, shit" behind Kirsten and Donny drew their attention. They pivoted at the same time to find a tall guy standing behind them. He was easily six-four. White-blond hair. Deeply tanned which stood out like a sore thumb in the middle of an Ohio November. Similar to Donny and Kirsten, the stranger was dressed in jeans, t-shirt, and an insulated denim jacket that had seen better days.

But it was the dangerous prickle of fae magick that set Kirsten's teeth on edge.

Donny growled deep in his chest. In her peripheral vision, fur sprouted on his cheeks.

"Look, I don't want any trouble," the fae said.

"Your queen's the reason my father's dead." Donny's words were barely intelligible thanks to his snout elongating as he spoke.

Kirsten stepped between Donny and the fae. "Hackles down, Fryer. This is the guy I'm supposed to be tutoring."

"Reed's an idiot to allow a fae in the school," Donny rasped.

"And Kaley's an idiot for not telling you he's here either." Kirsten placed her palm against Donny's chest. His pulse pounded against her hand. "All I'm asking is that you stand down as long as he's not slinging spells."

"First, he tells us how he crossed the county line." Donny's fur receded, but his golden irises and canine pupils glared at the fae.

"Actually, that's a good question." Kirsten turned back to face the fae. "No Unseelie individual, agent or representative of theirs is allowed in Holmes County. Not after the Winter Queen's representatives swore never to step foot in the county again. Not after the amendments to the International Council's Accords."

"The amendment doesn't apply to those of fae blood neither Court claims," the new boy said coolly. "My father was fae, my mother Normal. Are you telling me you don't know how the Winter Queen regards half-bloods?"

That explained how he got into Holmes County. It didn't mean he wasn't trouble.

Kirsten regarded him. "I do. I also know most half-fae will do just about anything to be accepted by their Court."

"Not all of us," he shot back. "But then I wouldn't expect a mere witch to understand. The real question for me is whether the principal sicced you on me on purpose."

She laughed. "That's giving Reed too much credit. I'm one of the top students, and I'm aiming to graduate valedictorian."

"Really?" An ugly smile filled his face. "And how many hexes did that take?"

Donny shoved his way between Kirsten and the half-fae. "You're just like every other fae no matter your bloodline, a conceited, full-of-yourself jerk." The were was angry, but he'd regained control of his human form.

The half-fae rolled his eyes. "Look, dude, I don't know you. I don't know your dad. And I sure as hell don't know the asshat who killed him. Like I said, I don't need the trouble." His sneaker squeaked when he pivoted, and he marched down the hallway.

Kirsten looked at Donny.

He met her gaze. "Is Reed crazy, or just that ignorant about supernaturals?"

"In our beloved principal's case, it's deliberate ignorance." She pressed her lips together and looked back down the hall, but the half-fae had turned the corner. "This is going to come back and bite me in the ass. I just know it." She slumped against the wall.

Kaley rushed up to them. "Sorry I'm late." She looked around. "Hasn't River shown up yet?"

"River?" Donny growled. "What kind of name is River?"

"There's the actor River Phoenix. And he was a Normal." Kaley frowned. "What did I miss?"

Donny glared at her. "Why didn't you tell me I was supposed guard your sister from an Unseelie?"

"I thought you knew about him," Kaley protested. "You were the one complaining about the honey scent in the air."

"For all I knew, Life Sciences was making baklava," he muttered. "If you knew the guy was fae, why the hell didn't you tell me?"

Kaley's mouth opened and closed a couple of times, but no explanation came out.

Donny turned to Kirsten. "Don't let Kaley dye her hair blond anymore. It's killing her brain cells."

"Hey!" Kaley protested, but Donny was already striding down the hallway.

"It doesn't matter," Kirsten murmured. "We need to find out who this River Martin's father is, and why River is in Millersburg in the middle of the semester. Unfortunately, I have basketball practice first."

She headed for the locker room. It was time to put the internship offer Uncle Jimmy, the Holmes County sheriff, and Millersburg Police Chief Hall made last month to the test. The real question was how to get rid of Kaley before heading to the sheriff's department headquarters.

Because her twin would definitely throw a fit if she knew Kirsten planned to ask Uncle Jimmy or Deputy Wolford to run a background check on River Martin.

Chapter 3

While Kirsten headed to the girls' locker room to change, Kaley strolled out to the football practice field with her backpack slung over her shoulder. She may not have Kirsten's brains, but neither did her sister have Kaley's social finesse. Kirsten had totally blown any chance of getting information from River Martin with her attitude.

But they wouldn't have too many more days of fairly decent weather. Not with the sun shining and the air warm enough to sit outside to study. With football over for the season, coming out to the practice field would provide her a little privacy to think about what to do regarding River.

Or it should have.

Another figure sat on one of the benches at the side of the field. A figure with a shock of white hair. Maybe the Goddess was giving her the chance to fix the situation. She headed toward River.

He looked up at the same time his magick jabbed at hers, and he slammed his textbook shut. "Aw, hell no!"

"Whoa, man." Kaley held up her palms. "I heard what happened. I came over to apologize. My sister was not born with any manners. Neither was my friend Donny."

He paused in shoving his textbook into his backpack, but his piercing blue eyes narrowed as he watched her. "And why should I trust a witch?"

"My dad says trust has to be earned." She looked across the brown, dormant grass of the field to the bare dark trees beyond before she returned her attention back to River. "He's a Normal, so I do understand a little of your position. Our coven constantly questions me and my sister. So, no, I don't expect you to trust me. Not until I've earned it."

"But your coven acknowledges you and your sister as witches though, right?" he said. The hint of jealousy in his voice brought out Kaley's sympathy.

"May I sit down with you in order to have a proper civil conversation?" Maybe using a more formal request would pacify him.

He shook his head. "Why are you trying to sound like my grandmother?"

"I was trying to remember my etiquette," she stated neutrally. Maybe Rain's father never explained the Court's behavior to him.

"All right." He scooted over on the bench. "But can you drop the weird act?"

"No problem." She straddled the bench so she could face him. The cold of the plastic-coated metal seat penetrated her jeans, but she did her best to ignore the discomfort. "Do you know about the Unseelie prohibition in Holmes County under the I.C. Accords?"

"Your sister informed me earlier." His cheeks flushed a light pink. "But technically, I've never read the Accords."

A thread of unease wound through Kaley. "Goddess, please tell me your fae parent told you about the International Council."

"Don't know my dad." Bitterness iced River's words. "He knocked up my mom in a one-night stand. Disappeared after that. She never saw him again. Mom's a Normal. So, no, he didn't tell me about the International Council."

Kaley stared at him. "Well, leaving you alone with Normals was a crappy thing to do. How did you find out you were part-fae?"

"I . . . did things." He stared at the tips of his athletic shoes. "When I was little. It wasn't until the Rainier Outing when I was in kindergarten that Mom figured out what my dad must have been. We've picked up a few things here and there since then."

The Outing. When the Normals discovered the existence of the supernaturals living among them. The covens and packs along the

Puget Sound banded together to save the innocent citizens who couldn't evacuate when Mount Rainier erupted, the volcano where Glass Lake was now.

"Wow," she said softly. "That must have been rough on both of you."

A derisive sound came from low in his throat. "You have no fucking idea."

"What brought you and your mom to Millersburg?"

"She grew up here." River looked up at her. "Her mother didn't want anything to do with us for years. She's pretty religious, and she acted like Mom had done something terrible when she got pregnant." A half-smile, half-grimace twisted his mouth. "It didn't help when she saw me stop a vase in midair I'd knocked over."

Kaley giggled. "I get that. We have to be on our super-best behavior around Grandma Wilson. No magick whatsoever." She sobered. "I don't get why you moved here three months into the school year."

"Mom got a big promotion about the same time her mom had some health problems. The promotion meant she could work from home except for going into the local Safewide Insurance office two days a week." He shrugged. "It happened pretty fast. We're staying at the Holiday Inn while her company packs up our house in Indianapolis."

"Man, that's got to suck leaving all your friends behind," Kaley murmured. She couldn't imagine what she'd do if Mom or Dad got a better job somewhere out of state. Or even another part of Ohio. She would throw a major fit if they had to move before graduation. But Kirsten would embrace such a development.

Life just wasn't fair.

"Yeah, it did." River grimaced. "Big time. Especially in the middle of high school."

"But you have heard of the International Council?"

He nodded. "Only a little bit. They're like the supernatural version of the United Nations, right?"

"Kind of. They have a little more bite than the U.N." Kaley smiled. "And in some cases, that's literally."

"The werecoyote with your sister outside of the library—" He paused as if he wasn't sure he wanted to broach the subject. "He said my kind killed his dad. Is that what you meant by these accords?"

"Sort of." She stared at the trees again, not sure why she suddenly felt uncomfortable. Maybe because it felt like she was accusing him personally. "Before I was born, there was a rash of Normal murders in Holmes County. They were committed by a wanagamesak—"

"A what?"

"A Native American water spirit. It got stuck." She linked her fingers together. "Bonded to the bones of the shaman of the tribe it protected. The Winter Queen's assassin cut a deal with Donny's dad for the shaman's bones, and therefore, control of the wanagamesak. The assassin made the wanagamesak kill people, including an Amish man whose sister was a highly placed enforcer with the Western U.S. Vampire Coven." She turned to River, watching his reaction. "When the Unseelie and the members of the Killbuck Pack got caught, the Winter Queen's assassin left Donny's dad to the vampires and their allies. He got his throat ripped out for kidnapping another werecoyote's pups."

River whistled softly and shook his head. "Sounds like his dad got what he deserved."

"Not disputing that." She shrugged. "Anyway, a local Normal attorney killed the assassin and negotiated the surrender and expulsion of the Unseelie who survived the fight. In the resulting political mess, the non-fae factions insisted on an amendment to the accords that no Unseelie of the Winter Court could step into Holmes County for as long as it existed."

"Wait." His white-blond eyebrows disappeared under his shaggy bangs. "A Normal killed a full-blooded fae?" Disbelief tinged his voice.

Kaley laughed. "Yeah, that shocked the crap out of everyone."

"So the accords..." River exhaled gustily. "That's why you looked totally freaked out this morning when I walked into homeroom."

"Yeah," she admitted.

Cold wind gusted across the field, ruffling their hair. Normally, she would have blocked the air without thinking about it, but the jangling edges of River's power against hers felt like a risk that wasn't worth the reward.

"Let's go inside," she suggested. "I'm not as smart as Kirsten, but if you can help me with trig, I can help you with everything else."

A faint smile crossed his face. "I don't know if I should be seen hanging out with the bad girl cheerleader."

"Excuse me?" Her voice rose.

He shrugged again before he stood. "I heard you took out the head cheerleader. That's the reason she's in the wheelchair."

"Oh, my Goddess!" Kaley jumped to her feet. "That is so not true!"

"So, you didn't kneecap her a la Tonya Harding?" he said. They walked toward the high school.

"Who's Tonya Harding?" She looked up at him. He was definitely teasing her, but she wasn't quite sure how to take it.

"A former Olympic skater." He glanced at her and grinned. "She was accused of being part of the plot to kneecap her biggest rival."

"In this case, Amelia did it to herself," Kaley grumbled.

"She deliberately took a steel pipe to her own knee?" Yep, he was definitely laughing at her.

Kaley stopped and whirled to face him.

River paused and looked back at her.

"She tried to hit me," Kaley ground out. "No magick. No tricks. I just ducked. She overbalanced and hit the concrete floor of the girls' locker room knee first. The Threefold Law applies to everyone, witch and non-witch alike. If she hadn't tried to pick a fight, she would have been fine."

"All right." He nodded. "The Normals are dangerous but stupid here. I'll keep that in mind." His cocky attitude made her laugh.

"C'mon. I'll buy you a pop." She beckoned, and they headed inside the school. For all of Mom and Jo's warnings, River didn't seem that dangerous. In fact, he reminded her of Donny. Someone trapped between two worlds and in desperate need of a friend.

Chapter 4

Kirsten impatiently tapped her fingers on the steering wheel of Mom's sedan. Where the heck was Kaley? Even if Kaley managed to talk her way into cheerleader practice, it had been cancelled at the last minute because Coach Cross developed the flu. Kirsten texted her sister. When Kaley didn't answer, Kirsten texted Donny, but he said Kaley hadn't grabbed a ride home with him.

For a split second, Kirsten imagined the new fae boy might have done something to Kaley, but she waltzed out of the front doors of the high school as if she didn't have a care in the world. As soon as Kaley slammed the passenger door shut, Kirsten threw Mom's car into gear and backed out of the parking space.

"What's the rush?" Kaley said as she buckled her seatbelt.

"Some of us have some errands to run." Kirsten glanced at her sister while she cruised across the lot to the driveway. "You want me to drop you at home first?"

"I thought we were picking up parts for the '69 on the way home."

Kirsten could hear the suspicion in Kaley's voice. She checked traffic both ways before she turned onto State Route 39 and headed into town.

"Look, I know the auto parts shop isn't your favorite place, or you would have answered my texts."

"I was helping someone with their homework." Kaley blushed.

Kirsten was about to make a snarky comment, but guilt mocked her. The principal had told her to help the fae kid, and she and Donny had only extended the old hostilities. "I'm sorry. I wasn't trying to dump my job on you."

"We weren't even born when the crap with the Unseelie went

down," Kaley said. "Neither was River or Donny. It doesn't help anyone if we hold on to our parents' feuds."

Kirsten braked at a red light. As much as she hated to admit it, Kaley was right. She hesitated a second before she said, "I'm sorry I was a jerk last night. I'll help you with trig when I get back from the parts store."

"Why are you insisting on taking me home—"

Kirsten could feel Kaley's gaze boring into her brain as the light turned green, and she pressed the accelerator.

"You're trying to ditch me because you're going to the sheriff's office, aren't you?" Kaley accused. "You want Julia to run a background check on River!"

"Since when are you on a first name basis with a fairy?" Kirsten checked her speed and eased up on the gas pedal. A speeding ticket through downtown wouldn't make a good impression on her future employers.

"That's racist, and you know it," Kaley spat.

"Oh, Goddess." Kirsten groaned. "What is it about you and strays?"

"When their own pack and court doesn't accept them, I am not piling on!"

"Fine. You can come with me to protect your man's honor."

"He's not my man." Kaley's cheeks told a totally different story. Her phone buzzed. She pulled it from her bag and checked the screen. "Why are you making a big deal about this?"

"I'm not the one who texted Jo first thing this morning about the fae," Kirsten grumbled.

"Half-fae," Kaley murmured as her thumbs danced across the glass of her phone.

"So that's how he was able to cross the county line." Kirsten tightened her grip on the steering wheel. It figured the Unseelie would find a loophole in the accords to slip an agent of theirs into Holmes County.

Kaley looked up from her phone. "Mom wants us both home."

Kirsten flipped the turn signal and tapped the brakes to turn into the sheriff's department parking lot. "Tell her we're on our way once we pick up Dad's order."

"I'm not lying for you," Kaley snapped.

"You want that help with trig?" Kirsten parked the car and turned to her sister.

"I'm already grounded." Kaley scowled at her.

"So, you can blame this on me." Kirsten yanked the car door latch. "Wait here."

But Kaley was already scrambling out of the car. "Oh, no, you don't. I'm coming with you."

"You said you didn't care about your man." Kirsten watched her sister across the roof of Mom's sedan.

"In the U.S., you're innocent until proven guilty." Kaley slammed the door. "And you're being a racist dick. Someone's got to defend River."

For some reason, her accusations sliced deep into Kirsten's soul. Was she treating River exactly like the Normals treated her ancestors? Burn them at the stake first and not even bother asking any questions?

"All right." She shrugged as they headed for the front door. "You can make sure we're doing this by the book."

Deputy Russ Collins sat at the duty desk. His freckled face lit up when they entered. "Well, if it isn't the Trouble Twins! What are you two doing here?"

Kirsten leaned on the counter. "Is Sheriff Birkheimer or Deputy Wolford here?"

"Sheriff just left on a call, but Julia's here." Russ held up his right index finger before he pressed a button on the huge phone set. "Deputy Wolford, you have visitors." The PA echoed through the building.

The phone set buzzed and a red light blinked. Russ picked up the handset. "Front desk." After a second, he winked at the girls. "Kirsten and Kaley Wilson." He hung up. "Go on back, ladies. You know the way, Kirsten."

He pressed another button and the steel door to the offices buzzed and clicked.

"Thanks, Russ." She waved, crossed the few steps to the door, and yanked it open. Kaley followed her into the back offices.

Kirsten stopped before the correct door and knocked.

A muffled "Come in" filtered from behind the wooden door. She turned the latch.

Julia Wolford sat at her desk. She was the daughter of Thaddeus Wolford, Jimmy's predecessor as sheriff. Like her dad, she was stockily built, but it was all muscle. Her medium brown hair was pulled into a tight bun. With her stepmom and stepbrothers being werecoyotes, she not only knew how to fight, but she fought dirty when she had to, as many criminal suspects had found out the hard way during her tenure as a law enforcement officer.

She paused typing on her keyboard and smiled. "Hey, girls! What's up?"

Kirsten shot a look at her sister before she said, "Is the joint supernatural taskforce aware a half-fae moved into Holmes County?"

Julia leaned back and folded her arms over her chest. "No." She cocked her head. "What about the accords? I thought fae were prohibited from coming here."

"The accords only apply to members of the Courts," Kirsten said.

Julia's lower jaw twitched. "So, only folks who are full-blooded fae."

"Yes." Kirsten nodded.

The deputy stared at the pile of paperwork on her desk a moment before she looked up again. "Could he be lying about being part-fae?"

"No." Kaley shook her head vigorously. "The word of a fae is like a Blood Seal for us witches. It's a magickal guarantee. They will literally be destroyed if they break their word."

"And for us, being around River is like bathing in poison ivy," Kirsten added.

"Innocent until proven guilty," Kaley snapped.

"It doesn't mean he's not up to something," Kirsten said.

"His mom's a Normal," Kaley bit back.

"A U.S. citizen?" Julia's attention flicked between Kirsten and Kaley.

"I don't know," Kirsten said at the same time Kaley said, "Yes."

Kirsten stared at her sister. "How would you know?"

"His mom was born and grew up here in Holmes County." Kaley scowled. "I actually talked to him instead of accusing him of shit like you and Donny did."

Kirsten tossed her hands up. "You're the one who raised the alarm this morning!"

"Maybe I was wrong." Kaley's fists clenched. "River's mom took a promotion back here because his grandmother isn't well."

Kirsten inhaled deeply and tried to relax the muscles in her own shoulders. "Maybe you're right, and he's telling you the truth. Or maybe he's here for another reason."

"Let me guess." An amused expression crossed Julia's face. "You want me to do a background check on this River and his mom."

Kirsten nodded. "Maybe find out who his dad is? And can we find out who his mom works for, too?"

"She works for Safewide," Kaley said.

"How did you find out?" Kirsten stared at her sister.

"I asked." Kaley glared back. "You know the proverb about flies and honey? Maybe you should try it some time."

"It depends on if the father is listed on this River's birth certificate. Ohio law won't let a woman put just any random guy's name on the paperwork." Julia shrugged. "And you're assuming River's mom knew his real name and face. If he wore a glamour . . ."

Kirsten hated to admit it, but the deputy was right. "The name he gave the school was River Martin."

Julia paused in writing down the name. "Wait. Any relation to Cissy Martin? The owner of The Hair and Now. Had a heart attack at the end of summer."

Kirsten turned to Kaley. "Well?"

She raised her hands. "Hey! I just talked to the guy while we did homework. I didn't take a complete family history."

Kirsten shoved her irritation down with a lot of effort. Her sister could be so frickin' air-headed at times. "You just said his mom took the position here partly because of his grandmother."

"But I don't know for sure if it's Cissy Martin." Kaley waved her hands. Her frustration slammed into Kirsten's psyche.

Kirsten inhaled deeply to calm herself. They were feeding off each other's emotions again. A problem at times while they were growing up. A comfort at others. But with puberty came distance as they each tried to deal with adulthood and the weird mix of emotions that came with the hormonal changes. Understanding the reasons didn't make the emotions any easier to deal with.

She turned back to Julia. "Can you see what you can find out? We'll talk with Mom and Jo about the situation tonight, and I'll call you with an update tomorrow."

The deputy smiled. "Sounds like a plan, but don't you two or your mom and aunt do anything in the meantime. Last thing, you guys need is a harassment complaint by the Martins."

Kirsten and Kaley both nodded.

Once they left the building and were settled in Mom's sedan, Kaley glared at Kirsten. "What the hell is wrong with you? You've bitched about Donny all these years, and now River?"

"You call me racist again, and I'll hex you with acne so bad you won't be able to show your face until next year."

"Then stop acting like one," Kaley snapped back.

Kirsten jabbed the button to start the car. She wasn't racist. Was she?

With Donny, it was complicated. He teased her unmercifully when they were little. Nor did she like the way he followed Kaley like a puppy. And Kaley led the poor guy on. It wasn't right.

But this River Martin? Her witchy sense was tingling. There was something more going on than a promotion and an elderly relative needing help. And darn it, she was going to find out what.

Chapter 5

Kaley remained silent on their ride to the auto parts store. Her sister's guilty-until-proven-innocent attitude was getting on her last nerve.

"You know I'm checking up on him after what happened seventeen years ago," Kirsten said softly. "The fae were behind those murders, and there hasn't been a fae in Holmes County since then until now."

"That all happened before we were even born," Kaley repeated for what felt like the one hundredth time this afternoon. She crossed her arms and stared at the passing businesses, but her sister didn't take the hint.

"And they have long lifespans and longer memories," Kirsten continued. "Mom and Jo sided with Fitz, Julia's stepmom and her family, and what was the Augustine coven against the Winter Queen's duke over the new goddess. What happens if the fae decide to punish our kids or grandkids because of what Mom did? What if the fae decide to take their anger over their dead out on us? Or Dad?"

Kirsten flipped the turn signal and pulled into the parking lot of the auto parts store.

Kaley waited until her sister parked before she said, "Have you noticed you hold Donny's dad against him unless you want something from him? It sounds more like you have a bad case of projection when it comes to holding grudges."

Kirsten stared at her with an open mouth until her cheeks darkened under the halogen safety lights blinking on along the exterior of the building. Her jaws snapped shut, and she yanked on the door latch.

"I'll be right back with Dad's order." She got out of the car and slammed the door shut a little harder than necessary before she stomped into the auto parts store.

Kaley slumped in the passenger seat. For someone so smart, her twin could be so damn stupid at times. Or was she using Donny's father simply as an excuse to keep the werecoyote at arm's length all these years? It may be hard as heck to read a were's mind, but their emotions resembled the neon lights of a big city. Now, that was an interesting possibility. Was Kirsten's attitude because she liked Donny and didn't want to admit it?

A flicker of movement in the side mirror caught Kaley's attention. The Painter Building directly across the street was an older three-story structure built prior to the First World War, and it had fallen into disrepair. The antique glass was intact but grimy, as was the brick exterior. The shoe store that had been its last business tenant closed ten years before she and Kirsten had been born.

There was definitely a person-shaped shadow near the front windows of the Painter Building. Kaley twisted in her seat to look through the rear window of Mom's sedan. Light flickered inside, but not enough to show details of the person behind the window. Was someone checking out the building? They'd need a flashlight with the electricity shut off.

No, the flicker looked like a live flame, but the wavy antique glass could be distorting things. Except the light seemed to grow as she watched it.

She yanked the latch and pushed open the car door. The acrid scent of smoke hit her nose, and not the good kind from a cookout. She pulled her phone from her pocket and dialed 9-1-1. Heart in her throat, she waited for the cell company operator to transfer her to the Holmes County operator.

"Holmes County 9-1-1. What is your emergency?" the operator chirped.

"The Painter Building's on fire." Kaley rattled off the street address for the auto parts store. "It's the old brick building across the street."

The operator's voice turned serious. "The fire department is on its way, ma'am. What's your name and number in case we get disconnected?"

Kaley opened her mouth to answer when the fire seemed to rush to the first floor front windows. Out of instinct, she raised her hands and threw up a ward. Her phone squealed and sparked from the magickal energy overloading its circuits, and it fell from her fingers.

Despite her protective wall of air and magick, the force of the explosion slammed her into the concrete wall of the auto parts store. She landed hard on the building's outside walkway, knocking the air from her lungs. Pain ripped through her right shoulder. Somehow, she curled into a fetal position and shielded her head with her arms as debris rained around her.

She was dimly aware of people shouting, but they sounded far away from the ringing in her ears. Two people crouched next to her. The ringing made it hard to concentrate, and it didn't help the ache in her head.

A blurry version of Kirsten appeared in front of her. "Kaley! Talk to me!" Her voice was muffled, as if she had to shout to be heard.

"You haven't listened to a damn thing I've said all evening," Kaley grumbled.

Kirsten's eyes glimmered with a liquid sheen. In the distance, something droned with a rising and falling sound. It finally registered in Kaley's rattled brain she was hearing the sirens of the approaching fire trucks.

She struggled to rise. "There was someone in the building."

"Stay still, honey. The ambulance will be here any minute." Hands pressed down on her right shoulder, and she cried out.

"What's wrong?" Kirsten demanded.

"M-my shoulder." Kaley tried to suck air past the agony in her joint, but the oxygen was tainted by the acrid smoke filling the air. "Kirsten, there's someone in there. In the Painter Building."

"Girl, that place has been abandoned for a couple of decades."

Kaley blinked and finally recognized the speaker as one of the guys who worked at the auto parts store. His balding head reflected the dancing red flames from across the street.

"You sure you saw someone in there?" Kirsten asked.

Kaley started to nod and thought better of it at the wave of dizziness. "Yes. I saw a shadow moving around on the first floor before I saw the flames. I climbed out of the car to double check before I called 9-1-1."

Kirsten stared over Kaley's head. "If there was someone in there . . . the building's fully engulfed."

Kaley's stomach wrenched. If someone was in the building, either they escaped before the explosion, or they were now barbequed.

Chapter 6

Kirsten leaned against the beige wall outside of the curtained section where her sister lay in the Pomerene Hospital emergency room. The smell of antiseptic was the same whether it was people medicine or pet medicine. A headache throbbed against the back of her skull and her right shoulder ached something fierce. It had been a long time since she'd felt her twin's pain. The resonance said just how bad Kaley was hurting. Kirsten listened as her sister repeated the same story about seeing someone inside the destroyed building before the fire started to the two police officers.

The paramedics at the scene insisted Kaley needed to go to the ER. She had multiple cuts and scrapes in addition to the sore shoulder, but they were most worried about her hitting her head when the blast knocked her into the exterior wall of the store. Kirsten followed the ambulance to the hospital. Thank Goddess, Mom had gotten the hands-free phone option when she chose the sedan. She was able to call Mom and Dad on the way.

"Kirsten!" Mom rushed up to her and wrapped her in a tight hug. "Are you all right?"

"I'm fine. I was inside the parts store, picking up Dad's order when the explosion happened." She lowered her voice. "The police are talking to Kaley now. She's the only one who got hurt."

"We saw your mother's car." Dad frowned.

"Really?" Kirsten stared at him over Mom's shoulder, a feeling of incredulousness wiping out her guilt over fighting with her twin before the accident. "That's what you're worried about? That damage wasn't our fault!"

"I know it wasn't, sweetheart." He wrapped his arms around both her and Mom. "All the dings scared the hell out of me when I saw it because your sister was hit by the same chunks of brick and mortar. If the explosion happened a couple of minutes later, we could have lost both of you."

Kirsten hadn't needed her parents to make her feel safe for a long time, but she was damn glad they were there now. Not to mention, it shook her how close Kaley had come to getting killed. The emotions she'd pushed down since she heard the explosion bubbled to the surface. Tears trailed down her cheeks.

"You two are finished." The loud, commanding voice from behind the curtain sounded like the ER nurse who was caring for Kaley.

Mom and Dad released Kirsten and stared at the curtain.

"We're questioning a key witness," one of the officers said.

"And I am taking *my* patient down to radiology. Do I need to call security because you're interfering with my care of a patient?"

The curtain hangers rattled as the nurse pushed the curtain back. Both police officers turned beet red when they realized the editor-in-chief of *The Millersburg Monitor* stood on the other side. The nurse and the orderly appeared totally amused.

"Hey, Mark. Lewis." Mom waggled her fingers before she turned to the nurse. "I'm Kaley's mom, Rachel Wilson. What are we looking at?"

"The doctor's ordered x-rays for both her head and her shoulder." The nurse smiled. "It's more of a precaution than anything. If you want to go to the waiting room, I'll let the doctor know you're here."

Mom and Dad brushed past the two officers. They each kissed Kaley gently on her forehead and murmured how much they loved her.

Meanwhile, Kirsten examined the nametags on the two officers. Hatfield and Zarnecki. From the questions they had been asking Kaley, they thought she'd caused the explosion and fire.

Guilty until proven innocent.

Damn, no wonder Kaley was pissed at her. She was acting as bad as the Normal cops.

"We'll be right here, sweetheart," Dad murmured.

"I know." Kaley's smile was a tepid version of the brilliant one she wore while cheerleading.

The nurse and the orderly raised the rails and unlocked the wheels of Kaley's hospital bed. Kirsten's heart gave a little jump when Kaley held out her left fist as she was wheeled toward Kirsten. She bumped her sister's fist with her own as the bed passed. Kaley and the orderly disappeared around the corner that led to the elevators.

Zarnecki, the cop Mom had addressed as Lewis, walked over to Kirsten. "You sure you didn't see anything, Miss Wilson?"

"Like I said before, I was inside the auto parts store when we heard the explosion." She shrugged. "Kaley was in the car waiting for me. Or I thought she was. When I saw her curled up on the pavement . . ." She let the tears she'd been holding in flow down her cheeks.

"Are you trying to say my daughters had something to do with that fire?" Dad growled.

"We have to look at every possibility," Hatfield, the cop Mom called Mark, said. "It's nothing personal, Doctor Wilson."

"Except we don't see you talking to anyone else who was in the store or at one of the nearby businesses." Mom smiled sweetly.

"None of the rest of those people can throw fireballs out of thin air," Lewis shot back.

"I can't throw fireballs," Kirsten said quietly. "Neither can Kaley."

Hatfield frowned. "I thought that was a witch talent."

"It is, but not every witch has mastery over every element," Mom said. "Why are you assuming a witch had to set the fire?"

The two cops exchanged odd looks before they turned back to

Mom. Zarnecki cleared his throat. "Like I said, we have to look at all possibilities." He eyed Kirsten. "Call the station if you think of anything you forgot to tell us." The tone of his voice insinuated there was a ton of stuff she hadn't told him.

She nodded. "I'll let Chief Hall know if I think of anything else."

Red flooded Zarnecki's cheeks, but Hatfield was obviously holding back a grin.

"Thanks for your cooperation, Miss Wilson." Hatfield touched the brim of his hat before he dragged his partner from the ER.

"What was that all about?" Dad murmured once the cops were out of earshot.

Mom made a low sound in her throat. "Lewis Zarnecki is a member of Humanity Now."

"What's that?" Kirsten asked.

"A group that thinks supernaturals shouldn't have civil rights and that we're not even human."

Dad shook his head. "That makes no sense. Even the fae are distant cousins. Otherwise, they couldn't have children with the rest of us."

Crap. In all the craziness of Kaley getting hurt, Kirsten forgot about the other wild thing that had happened.

"A half-fae boy started at the high school today," she blurted.

"And?" Dad said at the same time Mom said, "What!"

"Keep your voice down," Kirsten hissed. "A new kid showed up in Kaley's trig class this morning. He's only half-fae. That's how he got into the county, right?"

Mom made a face. "Under the amendments to the I.C. accords, he'd have to be less than a full-blood. Did he threaten Kaley?"

"Whoa." Dad laid his hand on Mom's shoulder. "Aren't you jumping to conclusions here?"

"Really?" Mom jerked away from him. "After all the animal mutilations you dealt with? After all the people in this county Duke Hoarancill ordered the wanagamesak to murder?"

"That was seventeen years ago, honey—"

"Oh, Goddess!" A look of horror swept over Mom's face. "What's his name?"

"River Martin." Kirsten shrugged. "Or that's the name he registered under at school."

"Didn't Cissy Martin's daughter and grandson move back here after Cissy had her heart attack?" Dad said.

Mom pinched the bridge of her nose. "Cissy gave Heather so much grief for getting pregnant from a one-night stand. I should have guessed there was more to the story."

"So, what do we do about this River?" Kirsten asked. "What if the Winter Queen manipulated his mother's boss so she moved back here?"

Mom lowered her hand. What little color she had in her pale face disappeared. "You're sure he's part fae?"

"Yeah." Kirsten hugged herself. She wasn't proud of her earlier behavior toward him, but she didn't trust him an inch either. And that crazy explosion and fire right after their confrontation? But she had no proof, and if she made random accusations, she was no better than Lewis Zarnecki. "I'm sure. You can ask Donny Fryer for verification."

"Let me talk to some people before we do anything," Mom said.

"You two sound as bigoted as Lewis," Dad pointed out, looking at them each in turn. "What happened to innocent until proven guilty? It still applies in this county to everyone."

"You don't understand, Ethan—"

"Everyone, Rach." Dad enunciated each syllable slowly and clearly. "Else we're no better than Lewis and the idiots from Humanity Now."

Mom grimaced, but she held up her palms in surrender. "Okay. Fine." She sucked in a deep breath and released it. "What do you propose?"

"If Kirsten is serious about interning with Jimmy come New Year's, this may be a good time for her to do some volunteer work." Dad grinned and winked at her.

"Then I guess we need to get the '69 on the road." Kirsten grinned back.

Chapter 7

Several hours after being poked and prodded and photographed, Kaley tried not to howl in agony while Kirsten helped her into a light summer nightgown once they were home. Instead, Penn yowled from where he sat on her pale pink comforter. Her familiar was definitely picking up her emotions, which was almost as bad as her twin sister doing it.

The docs at the hospital had diagnosed her with a concussion and a cracked right shoulder blade. They couldn't give her anything stronger than ibuprofen or acetaminophen for the pain thanks to the brain injury. The over-the-counter stuff wasn't making a difference.

"I'm sorry. I'm sorry," Kirsten repeated over and over again. Moisture gathered in her eyes. She had Kaley step into the nightgown for the minimum of moving her arm, but even the feather-light spaghetti strap shot agony through her shoulder.

And here, she thought the sling was bad.

"Crap," Kirsten muttered. "This isn't going to work." She carefully lowered both straps.

"Just pull up the left one," Kaley said.

As Kirsten did that and helped her put the sling back on, Mom came into Kaley's bedroom with extra pillows under her arms. "I'll call in a healer from Cleveland." She dropped her load on Kirsten's bed and began arranging them so she could sleep in a semi-upright position.

"By the time they get here, I'll be okay." Kaley tried to smile, but she knew it was a pretty pathetic attempt. "No sense wasting the gas or the healer's energy."

Kirsten opened her mouth, probably to argue, when rapid-fire knocking echoed through the house.

"Ethan!" Mom called.

"I got it!" Dad shouted.

Male voices rumbled up the stairwell from the foyer. Then Dad shouted again, "Kaley, Josh Fairbanks is here. You feel up to company?"

Kaley wanted to howl for a different reason. Of all the times for Josh to find his balls.

Kirsten smirked, which meant she'd picked up on Kaley's change of mood. "I'll dig out an air mattress and grab my comforter." She charged out the bedroom door, but everyone could hear her yell down the stairs, "Give her a sec to get decent, Josh!"

Mom pursed her lips at Kirsten's act and eyed Kaley. "Only for a few minutes."

"Don't worry." Kaley bit her lower lip as Mom helped her sit on the edge of the stuffed armchair she'd gotten from Grandma Wilson when she and Grandpa moved to a smaller house. The fabric background was beige with yellow birds and pears. It clashed with the multiple shades of rose in which she'd decorated her bedroom, but it was the chair Grandma had sat in when reading to her and Kirsten when they were little.

Mom grabbed the quilt at the end of Kaley's bed and draped it over her left shoulder and across her body. "You know, normally, I wouldn't let a boy up here in your room."

Kaley smiled at the teasing. "I know, but honestly, I do have a headache tonight."

They both giggled at the bad joke.

Mom leaned over and kissed her forehead. "Like I said, just a few minutes. You need some rest." She left.

Kaley wanted to lean back in the chair, but that would hurt more than sitting ramrod straight. She wasn't sure how she would be able to sleep through the night. This was worse than being grounded. She'd never complain about her punishment again.

Heavy footfalls hit the steps and were followed by rapping on her doorjamb. Penn leapt off the comforter and dove under the dust ruffle. Josh peered around the corner, his tousled brown hair falling into his eyes.

"Hey, Kaley."

"Hey yourself." She made a face. "Let me guess. Your dad was listening to the police scanner again."

"How'd you know?" He grinned and stepped into her room. "When you didn't answer my texts, I got worried and drove over to the hospital. They said you'd been released."

"I'm fine." She smiled, or tried to, past the pain. "Sorry I didn't answer. I dropped my phone when I got blown over. It's fried. Trust me. A real explosion is nothing like what they show on the movies."

"Ouch." Josh crossed to her bed and perched on the edge of the mattress. "You're not coming to school tomorrow, are you?"

"Not with a concussion and a broken right scapula." She grimaced. "I'll be out for the rest of the week. Probably won't be cheerleading for the next six weeks either."

"That's a sucky way to end your junior season." He hesitated a moment. "Maybe I could bring a movie and a pizza over on Friday. If you're feeling better, that is."

A warm feeling flooded her. Maybe she should have tried to get blown up sooner to get Josh's attention. She smiled, a real one this time. "That would be nice."

He stood and stepped closer to her. She lifted her head. The shyness descended over him, and he settled for a kiss on her cheek.

Someone cleared their throat from the doorway.

Josh jumped back and straightened at the same time. Kirsten stood there, the air mattress case slung over her left shoulder and her own purple comforter tucked under her right arm, all while trying to project an air of innocence.

"Ah, I'll call you tomorrow, Kaley. G'night." Josh rushed out of her bedroom like his hair was on fire.

Which if he got out of line with her, Mom probably would throw a fireball at him.

Kaley scowled out her sister. "Why do you have to act like such a jerk?"

"I wasn't the one making out after nearly dying." Kirsten scowled right back. "And some of us have to go to school tomorrow."

"You could sleep in your own room, you know," Kaley muttered. She wanted to stand up and stalk out, but with the dizziness, she knew she wouldn't make it the few steps to her bed, much less down the stairs.

Kirsten dumped her load on the floor next to Kaley's dresser. "There's no sense making Mom or Dad come all the way up here to check on you every couple of hours. We're not babies."

Guilt mixed with the pain and the need to go to the bathroom.

"Here, let's get you across the hall." The change in Kirsten's demeanor meant she was picking up Kaley's emotions.

"We've always been able to do that." Kirsten answered the unspoken question. She carefully removed the quilt and laid it across the foot of Kaley's mattress. "Right now, I really wish I had the true healing gift."

"Not every water witch has that particular talent." Kaley gritted her teeth as Kirsten helped her to her feet. "No sense feeling guilty over it."

"Guilt isn't the word for it." Kirsten kept to baby steps as they maneuvered out of the bedroom and to the bathroom.

Well, it wasn't a bathroom originally. The space had been the fourth upstairs bedroom, but the owners of the house before Mom and Dad had renovated the place. And the twins' parents let them paint the room a calming turquoise instead of the butt-ugly yellow color it had been. Kaley may be an air witch, but there were certain shades of her element's color the human eye should not be exposed to.

For all her griping about sharing a bathroom with her twin over the years, Kaley was thankful they had their own. She didn't think she could make it up or down the stairs by herself. With a whole room, there was plenty of space around the toilet for them to maneuver. It was more humiliating than Kirsten helping her wash her face and brush her teeth.

"You would do the same for me," Kirsten murmured as she patted Kaley's mouth dry.

"Would you please stop reading my mind?" But there was no real bite in her words.

"I wish I could shut you out." Kirsten shot her a rueful smile. "And believe me, I've been trying."

Kaley took another dose of extra-strength ibuprofen. "This is the pain talking, but why are you so afraid of liking Donny?"

"What? You think I have feelings for the runt. That's ridiculous." But Kirsten suddenly busied herself with hanging up Kaley's towel.

"My sister, ladies and gentlemen, Cleopatra, queen of denial." Kaley giggled.

"That's not funny." Kirsten wouldn't meet her gaze though as she tucked the bottle of ibuprofen in her pocket. "Let's get you in your bed and get the air mattress inflated, then I'll run downstairs and get you a water bottle to wash down your pills during the night."

In other words, she was hoping Kaley would fall asleep before she returned.

Kaley sighed. As much as she wanted to tease her twin, doing so wouldn't get Kirsten to admit she was attracted to the werecoyote.

When they entered her bedroom again, she thought for a split second she saw a distorted reflection of herself in the window. But Kirsten froze beside her, and the shadow's hair was too white under the moonlight filtering through the bare branches. The figure perched in the old maple outside of her bedroom window reached out and gently rapped on the glass.

Chapter 8

What the hell! Blood roared in Kirsten's ears. Why was River Martin in the maple tree in their front yard?

He reached out and knocked lightly on the glass again.

"Get me over to my bed and let him in before he falls out of the tree," Kaley murmured.

"Are you insane?" Kirsten hissed.

"No," Kaley snapped. "I'm tired and sore, and I'm not happy every guy in school wants to see me in my nightgown."

Kirsten held up her left index finger to signal River to wait. She shuffled along with Kaley's careful steps until they reached the bed. Once Kaley was seated, Kirsten draped the quilt back over Kaley's uninjured shoulder.

Penn, Kaley's golden tabby, poked his head from beneath the pale pink dust ruffle. He sneezed once before he slunk the rest of the way out from under the bed. He stalked over to the window before he looked over his shoulder expectantly at Kirsten.

A split second of hesitation fell over Kirsten. If she let the fae boy in, would it negate the protection wards Mom had on their house? Would Mom come racing up here demanding to know what was going on?

Worse, would Dad come up with a shotgun, pissed because she let a boy into Kaley's bedroom after hours?

Shoot, it wasn't like they were going to have a threesome or something.

She raised the sash. Thank goodness, the original windows had been replaced with modern double-paned insulated ones. The sash slid silently upward. She moved out of the way as River slung one long leg over the sill and worked the rest of his tall, lanky form into the house. He slid the sash back down and turned to Kirsten.

He was dressed in the same clothes and jacket he had on earlier at school. His white hair stood up in crazy angles and tufts like he'd been running his fingers through it. Penn purred and rubbed his body against the fae's jeans.

"Why haven't you healed Kaley?" River whispered.

"I don't have that talent," she said.

"But . . . you're a water witch?"

Kirsten rolled her eyes. "Are all fae this misinformed about us?"

"As misinformed as you witches are about me," he shot back.

"Stop it," Kaley said. "He's never had anyone to properly educate him." She looked up at River. "What are you doing here anyway?"

"I felt your pain at our hotel room." He shoved his hands into his coat pockets. "It wasn't stopping, so I couldn't sleep. Once Mom was snoring, I got dressed and came over here."

"You couldn't use the front door like a proper person?" Kirsten said.

"Given your attitude toward me, I figured your parents would be worse."

Kirsten jammed her fists on her hips. "Look there's nothing you can do, so why don't you go back home, and leave us be."

River ignored her, took a couple of steps, and knelt before Kaley. Penn stalked after him, leapt up on the mattress next to Kaley, and sat with his tail curled around his front paws.

"I can help you if you let me," River said.

Alien magick spiked painfully against Kirsten's shields. "Stop!" Realizing how loud that came out, she lowered her voice. "Do you know what happens when you mix witch and fae magick?"

He looked up at her. "Yeah, I do." He turned back to Kaley. "I need you to hold very still and not react to what you feel from me. I won't hurt you. I promise."

"You can't do this," Kirsten protested. "Not only will you kill her and yourself, you'll probably blow up our house, too."

Kaley glared up at her. "Just because I have a concussion doesn't mean I can't speak for myself." She looked at River. "What are you going to do?"

"Heal you," he said softly.

"You can't be serious." Fear twisted into anger, and Kirsten shoved River away from her sister. He landed with a muffled thud on Kaley's neon pink fake fur rug. Penn yowled.

"You have no right to harm her," Kirsten spat. "You even told her you weren't properly trained."

"Stop it, Kirsten," Kaley hissed. "I trust him, and it's my life, not yours."

"What about what you said to Mom?" Kirsten jabbed an index finger in the direction of Mom and Dad's bedroom downstairs. "You said you didn't want a healer to waste the energy."

"River drove across half of Millersburg, not two hours from Cleveland." Kaley swallowed hard. "I'm not going to get any sleep tonight if we do nothing. I trust him."

A questioning meow made Kirsten turn toward the doorway. Teller, her own gray tabby peered around the edge of the doorjamb. With a few bounds, he landed on the mattress. He padded over to sit next to his brother Penn, who nuzzled Teller's ear. It almost looked like he was whispering to the other cat.

About her.

River pushed himself back to his knees in front of Kaley.

Kirsten's shoulders sagged. "All right, but don't make me say I told you so."

Teller jumped down from Kaley's bed. He stalked over to Kirsten and butted her shin with his head. She could take a hint.

Kirsten scooped Teller into her arms and retreated to the ugly yellow chair of Grandma Wilson's that her sister insisted on keeping. She sat down. Teller rubbed his cheek against hers.

"I hope you're right," she mumbled. Teller curled up on her lap and purred.

"Like I said, don't react," River murmured.

"I won't." The smile Kirsten graced him with was a little brighter than the one she gave Josh. Her smile would have been a lot more brilliant if it weren't for the dark circles that smudged the skin beneath her eyes.

River placed his hands on Kaley's knees. The prickles of fae magick grew sharper. It took everything Kirsten had not to react either. She glanced at Penn, but the gold tabby merely cocked his head and watched the pair with a curious expression.

A purplish-blue glow surrounded Kaley. Her eyes rolled back, and she fell over on her side. Kirsten winced, expecting a wave of pain, but if anything, her right shoulder no longer pulsed with the sympathy ache from her sister. However, her head still throbbed, probably a residual effect from Kaley's injuries. Penn rose on all fours, padded closer to Kaley's head, and sniffed her cheek.

The glow faded, and Kaley began to snore. River let go of her knees and stood.

The one small favor was the house hadn't blown up from any magickal interaction.

Teller jumped down from Kirsten's lap and stalked over to Kaley's bed. He leapt up on the mattress and joined his brother in checking out Kaley. After a few seconds, the cats seemed satisfied. Teller jumped back to the floor and stretched.

With the prickle of fae magick fading, Kirsten stood and crossed to Kaley. She shook her sister, but there was no response. However, Kaley's face was no longer pinched in pain. Kirsten eased the quilt out from under her sister, lifted Kaley's legs so they were on her bed, and spread the quilt over her.

Kirsten looked up at River. His face appeared green-gray beneath his tan.

"Are you okay? You look like you're about to pass out."

"I'll be fine," he murmured. "Just give me a minute."

"But why did Kaley pass out?"

"For me, a healing takes energy from both me and the person I'm trying to heal." He looked at Kaley and back at Kirsten. "Doesn't it work the same way for witches?"

"Yeah." She glared at him. "But I've never seen someone pass out from a healing before. Sleep it off, but not keel over like she did."

"She was hurt worse than the doctors said." River swallowed hard. "She had bleeder in her brain."

Kirsten brushed past him and laid her palm on Kaley's forehead. Her sister's skin was icy to the touch. "What else did you do to her?"

"I lowered her body temperature a bit to reduce the swelling. She needs the sleep to finish the repairs." He headed for the window, but not before an odd expression crossed his face.

Kirsten followed him, unsure of what else to do.

River raised the sash, and cold November air blasted into the room. He swung his right leg over the sill.

"You realize if she doesn't wake up in the morning, I'll hunt you down," she said.

He looked at her with his intense pale blue eyes. "I know," he said solemnly before he maneuvered the rest of his body out of the window. He grabbed a thin but sturdy branch. The maple limb bent as if it were aware of the fae and lowered him to the yard. When he released it, the branch didn't snap into place. It slowly returned to its original position.

Under the street lights, River nodded once to her before he seemed to turn into a dark form that sank into the bigger shadow of the old maple and disappeared.

Chapter 9

Light streamed through Kaley's window the next morning. At least, she thought it was the next morning.

Something felt wrong, but Penn was curled up next to her on her pillow. She rolled over under the quilt Grandma Wilson had made her, not her comforter. What had she done last night?

The explosion and fire at the Painter Building.

She jerked upright. There was still a dull ache in her shoulder, and she wore the sling the ER doctor sent her home with, but her head didn't feel like it was about to fall off her neck. There was a purple sticky note with Kirsten's neat script in the spot where her phone normally sat.

Use Mom's phone to text me when you wake up.

Kaley read the note again. Text her? On Mom's phone? Oh, that's right. Her own phone had smashed to bits on the exterior wall and concrete walkway of the auto parts store. Just like her skull had almost been smashed.

She reached for the back of her head. No lump. No headache. No dizziness. Her shoulder was a bit stiff, which it would be after a healing.

Healing?

River had been in the old maple tree outside her window last night, but everything else was a blur. Or had she dreamed about him?

If she hadn't . . .

Oh, Goddess. What story did Kirsten tell Mom and Dad this morning? Or worse, had she narced about River sneaking into Kaley's room last night? The most damaging problem would be if Mom or Dad had caught River in her room after she had passed out.

Last thing she needed was to have her grounding extended.

She swung her legs over the side of the bed and looked around her room. The air mattress still lay inflated on the floor with Kirsten's pillow and comforter. Teller curled up on top of the purple comforter, the tip of his tail covering his nose. Kirsten stayed in Kaley's bedroom and was supposed to wake her up every two hours. Yet, she didn't remember Kirsten checking on her last night.

Her curtains were partially closed. She tried to pull last night from her recalcitrant brain. River had been perched in the tree when Kirsten helped her back from the bathroom. She'd given him permission to heal her. Then, nothing.

She removed her sling and stretched her arms over her head.

The better question was what she would tell Mom when she went downstairs. She had no doubt Mom had stayed home. Dad couldn't exactly work from home because Mom would never allow barnyard critters in her house.

First of all, if she were still hurting, she wouldn't get dressed. She reluctantly put the sling back on and managed to get her left arm into the sleeve of her bathrobe. It took a couple of tries to fling the right side of her robe over her right shoulder.

Penn opened one eye and peer up at her. He seemed satisfied because he snuggled over on the warm spot on her mattress and partly under her covers. Teller, on the other hand, didn't so much as twitch from the air mattress. Either Mom or Kirsten must have fed the cats. Otherwise, they would have been patting her face and meowing long before now.

Feeling a bit off center with the sling on, Kaley eased down the stairs and shuffled through the living room.

". . . Cory, I need the shots of the Painter Building by one. I've got an interview with Fire Chief Nicholls at two," Mom said. "She's battered but okay. I'm more worried about a member of Humanity Now like Zarnecki being assigned to the case."

Kaley stepped into the dining room. Sure enough, Mom had her phone glued to her ear while she spoke with her staff photographer. She looked up from her laptop, smiled, and held up her left index finger.

There was a pause as Cory spoke before she said, "No, by phone. I need to stay home with Kaley today. Just e-mail them to me." She lowered the phone and tapped the screen to end the call. "How are you feeling this morning, sweetheart?"

"Better than I did last night." Which was the truth. "Kirsten left me a note to text her when I woke up. May I borrow your phone for a sec?"

"Sure." Mom handed her the device. Her attitude was a total one-eighty from two days ago when Kaley had been busted for skipping a stupid study hall. "What would you like for breakfast? Eggs? French toast?"

"Actually, can I have some oatmeal?" Kaley sat down heavily at the dining room table. "My stomach's still feeling a little queasy." Which was also true.

"Coming right up."

Once Mom was safely in the kitchen, Kaley tapped out a message.

Thanks for staying with me last night.

Mom's phone displayed that Kaley's message had been read, and an answer was being typed. The phone beeped, and a blue conversation bubble appeared on the screen.

Like I told M&D, getting up with u every 2 hrs is practice for when I have a baby.

Kaley snickered. Talk about a distraction technique. But at least, she knew the story Kirsten stuck with this morning. Kaley's thumbs danced across the screen.

Can u get my homework assignments?

Once again, she waited. At the beep, the blue bubble popped up again.

No problemo!

The message was followed by three smiley faces.

Kaley set the phone next to Mom's laptop. So, River Martin was a healer. That was as rare a gift among the fae as it was among witches.

She wasn't a fool to think he'd told her everything about himself yesterday. But why would he have felt her pain from the explosion? Kirsten made sense because they were identical twins. So identical, Kaley made a point of dying her hair blond since seventh grade just so people didn't assume she was Kirsten.

Even Mom or Jo sensing her pain made more sense because they were family. But River . . .

There were other people suffering in this town worse than Kaley. Miz Rose had arthritis like a lot of older folks in town. River's own grandmother had a heart attack. Heck, driving to the hospital last night might have been like catnip to River with all the people in pain there.

Or was River's talents the real reason his mom wanted to move back to Millersburg? Did she know about his gift and wanted to heal her own mother?

"Penny for your thoughts?" Mom walked into the dining room with a steaming bowl. She set it in front of Kaley. "It looked like you were a million miles away."

"Thanks for making me breakfast." Kaley swirled the spoon with her left hand to mix the oatmeal, brown sugar, and splash of milk. She wasn't sure she could keep up the charade of still being injured. "I guess I was."

"You want to talk about it?" Mom sat down in front of her laptop again.

"That depends." Kaley took a quick bite of her oatmeal and swallowed the warm cereal. "Are you going to go ballistic like Kirsten did?"

"Ah, so it's about the fae boy." Mom glanced at her laptop screen before she looked back at Kaley. "Honey, I know you might feel certain . . . urges toward this boy—"

"Oh, geez, Mom!" Her spoon splashed back in her bowl. "I'm seventeen, and I know about sex. He didn't glamour me or use a love spell. He couldn't without killing himself in the process."

She stared at the ceiling for a moment, trying to find the right words to get through to Mom. "Look, I know you and Jo have history when it comes to the fae. I get it. I really do. But why is everyone assuming River is part of the Winter Queen's court? That he's here to make trouble? It's not his fault some asshole knocked up his mom."

"Sweetheart, I know you want to believe that, but—"

"But what?" Kaley waved her left hand. "How would you like it if the farmers around here started blaming you for their cows not giving milk or their crops failing?"

Mom cleared her throat. "That's not the same thing—"

"Isn't it?" Kaley's eyes stung. "You haven't even met this guy. And you want to play judge, jury, and executioner!"

"You didn't see the bodies!" A wave of power emanated from Mom. Kaley's skin prickled at the heat, and the chandelier swayed and tinkled above them.

Mom trembled, and she clenched both fists to bring her power back under control. "You didn't see what the Winter Queen's assassination team did to the animals and the people in this county."

"Has it occurred to you that River and his mom are just as much victims of that fae bullshit as everyone else? That maybe the Unseelie assassination team abused River's mom? What if she was raped and her own mother kicked her out because she got pregnant?"

Mom took a deep breath and released it. "Maybe you're right."

"Look, I know I'm still grounded but once that's done, can I please invite River over for dinner?" Kaley tried her best puppy dog eyes at Mom. "So you can meet him and see what he's really like?"

"I-I'll think about it," she murmured.

"And talk it over with Dad?" Kaley prompted, though from Mom's reaction, she had a pretty good idea Dad would go along with it.

Mom sighed. "All right, you two win."

"We two?" Kaley cocked her head. "Did Kirsten say something?"

Mom made a face. "No, your father also said to invite him over." The idea that Dad would suggest such a thing made Kaley want to dance around the dining room. Instead, she said, "Oh, okay," and dug into her oatmeal.

Chapter 10

Kirsten stared at her physics assignment during study hall, but nothing made sense. Her mind kept replaying last night. The texts from Kaley were reassuring, but they didn't answer two very important questions. Who had Kaley spotted inside the Painter Building prior to the fire? And why had River Martin felt the pain from her injuries?

Someone dropped into the seat across the table from her and jerked her out of her circular thoughts. She looked up to find River Martin.

"Since you didn't hunt me down, I'm assuming Kaley's feeling a lot better." His demeanor was deadpan, not self-satisfied. It only served to irritate her further.

"You two took an awful chance last night," Kirsten murmured.

"You didn't stop us," he said.

"She didn't stop what?" Hope Stillwell plunked herself down next to River at the same time Donny Fryer slid into the seat next to Kirsten.

"This guy bothering you again?" While Donny's words were directed to her, his attention was focused solely on River.

"Stop it," Kirsten ordered. "All of you."

Mrs. Price glared at them from across the room.

Kirsten's phone vibrated in her pocket. She pulled it out and read the text from Julia Wolford.

Favor Xchange. Can u and DF meet me and the fire chief at the Painter Building after school?

Kirsten knew Julia would call in the favor she owed the deputy for running the background check on River, but she didn't expect it this soon. She turned the phone so Donny could read it. "You in?"

"Sure." He looked up at her. "But you've got a game tonight, and why would Deputy Wolford want me?"

Kirsten looked around her. No one else was close enough to hear, but she still lowered her voice. "Because she trusts her stepbrothers, and you aren't part of the Killbuck pack."

"Oooo!" Hope grinned maniacally. "Can I come, too?"

"Where are we going?" River said.

Kirsten hesitated. The way he'd shifted into shadow sounded a lot like what Kaley described seeing inside the Painter Building last night.

Right before the explosion that nearly killed her.

Maybe the truth would work better in shaking something loose from River than a lie. "This isn't a field trip. The sheriff and police chief have asked me to join a special taskforce after I graduate. But they must have found something funky at the site of the Painter Building explosion and fire because they asked for my help."

"And your pet 'coyote's?" River gestured at Donny who growled low in his throat.

Under the table, Kirsten laid a hand on Donny's thigh. He remained tense, but the slight sheen of fur on his exposed skin disappeared.

She cocked her head and smiled at River. "I wouldn't say things like that in front of Deputy Wolford. She adores her stepbrothers, and all three of them are werecoyotes."

Rain's mouth twisted as if he were trying not to laugh. "Point taken. What if I helped, too?"

"And why would you do that?" Kirsten said.

"Because the one person in this town who's treated me with a modicum of common courtesy got hurt by whoever started that fire." Rain's irises darkened to a deep blue. "If I can help, then I'm coming."

"I don't have any superpowers, but I'm coming, too," Hope said.

"You'll need someone to take notes, and I can spreadsheet your guys' impressions."

Kirsten turned to Donny. "Well?"

He shrugged. "It's your call. You're the one Sheriff Birkheimer and Chief Hall recruited."

She looked at River again. His aura remained steady, other than the deepening of the blue color just like his eyes.

"All right, you two can come." She held up her right index finger when both Hope and River opened their mouths. "On the condition you do what I say. I'm not losing my internship over either of you doing something stupid."

Hope nodded eagerly. After a pause and a glare that was definitely resentment, River gave Kirsten a single curt nod.

She tapped out a reply to Julia.

Got two extra volunteers. Hope S. and new fae. Alright?

A few seconds later, her phone buzzed with Julia's reply.

K (???)

Yeah, Kirsten would definitely have to explain to Julia why she let River tag along.

Her phone buzzed again, but this text was from Mom. Kirsten swallowed hard, fearing the worst. But the text was actually from Kaley.

It's K. When you see River, tell him he's invited over for supper.

Dad and Kaley must have been working on Mom hard to get her to agree to that. But since Kaley was using Mom's phone, it would be best not to ask too many questions.

When?

"Is the deputy arguing about Blondie and me coming with you?" River asked.

Kirsten looked up from her phone in time to see Hope slug River in the bicep.

"My name's Hope, doofus," she said. "And you're blonder than I am."

"No, it's a text from Kaley," Kirsten answered.

"Is she okay?" both River and Donny asked at the same time.

Her phone beeped. "Give me a second, would you?" She looked at the screen.

> Tonight after the game if he can. The parents picking up McKelvey's pizza.

Kirsten typed in her response. It would be rude not to invite the two people sitting with her and River.

> Is it okay if Donny and Hope come over, too? They're both sitting with us in study hall.

There was a long pause before Kaley texted back.

> Mom says OK.

Kirsten breathed a sigh of relief. Mom understood the need for some buffering when it came to River, and she trusted Donny to watch their backs.

"Since you're helping with my investigation, all three of you are invited to Casa Wilson for pizza after the girls' varsity game tonight," Kirsten said.

"McKelvey's?" Hope asked with an anticipatory gleam.

"Is there any other kind?" Kirsten said in mock dismay.

"What's a McKelvey?" Confusion covered River's face.

"Only the best pizza in Ohio ever." Donny grinned.

"We'll meet in the student parking lot by my car ten minutes after the final bell," Kirsten said.

"Yes, sir!" River saluted her, which prompted a very loud "SHHHH!" from Mrs. Price.

While the other three tried to stifle their snickers, Kirsten tried to quell her unease. Had she done the right thing when she agreed to River tagging along?

Chapter 11

Kaley lounged on the living room couch with the cats. She curled underneath her fuzzy pink Barbie blanket she'd had for years and was binging on her favorite series when Dad came in the front door. In his hand, he had a bag with a familiar telecomm logo.

"How you feelin', sweetheart?" He grinned.

"Two of Jared Padalecki is always a good thing." She smiled into return and hit the pause button on the remote. Maybe she was starting to get a handle on using her left hand for little tasks. "But the dizziness and headache have gone away. You're home early."

"Just stopping in on my way out to the Zimmer farm. One of their milk cows has developed mastitis." He sat beside her and handed her the bag. "Thought this might brighten your day."

Kaley laid the bag on her lap and pulled out the box with her left hand. "A new phone?"

"You still have your old number, but the tech couldn't save any of your contacts or apps. You'll have to reprogram it, but it'll give you something to do while you're laid up at home for the rest of the week."

Teller opened one eye, checked if the thing Kaley held was edible, and promptly went back to sleep. Penn rose and stretched before he began sniffing the box. Finally, he rubbed his cheek on the corner and purred.

"Ethan!" Mom leaned against the doorjamb between the living room and dining room, her arms folded and the reprimand clear in her voice. "I thought we were waiting until after her grounding was over."

"That's why I got the insurance." He shrugged. "For a situation like this. Nothing out of pocket. Officially, she dropped it."

"Uh-huh." Mom smiled and shook her head. "Not like the explosion and fire were all over the news."

"Technically, I did drop my phone when the blast threw me into the wall of the auto parts shop," Kaley said.

Mom and Dad ignored her.

"The explosion wasn't Kaley's fault, and I'm not punishing her for that," Dad said crossly. "We're damn lucky she wasn't hurt worse than she was."

Guilt poured through her at Dad's words. Mom was already freaked out about a fae in town, but Dad would go ballistic about a boy being in her room late at night. It didn't matter if she was less than a year from becoming a legal adult. Besides, Dad probably thought he could take out River. The story about Colin Fitzgerald, a local Normal attorney, killing the Winter Queen's assassin in a duel almost twenty years ago had become a legend in town.

Though most people left out the part the groundhog hole played in Mr. Fitzgerald's victory.

Maybe she should wait until after Mom met River. Kaley considered her idea. Even better, maybe he should pretend to heal her before supper. Yeah, that sounded like a better plan.

As long as she could convey her plan to Kirsten and River before they got here. Which meant the Goddess was smiling on her by having Dad get her a new phone earlier than expected.

Kaley gingerly opened the box. Not only was it a new phone, it was the latest model. She looked up at Dad. From Mom's angle, she couldn't see his wink.

"Thanks, Dad." Kaley swallowed hard. The gift meant he'd forgiven her, but that added to her pile of guilt. "I'll try not to disappoint you again."

"Honey, you've never disappointed me." He squeezed her foot beneath her fuzzy blanket before he looked over at Mom. "Did you hear from the coven?"

"The Water Elder said the soonest she could send someone down here was Friday." Mom's irritation was clear in her tone.

Dad snorted. "Then what's the point? Kaley will be fine by the end of the week."

Kaley winced. Goddess, she hated keeping secrets from her parents.

"When was the last time she took a painkiller?" Dad asked. He must have assumed she was in pain.

"Ten this morning." Mom frowned. "That's the reason the bottle is—" She rolled her eyes. "Sorry, sweetie. I wasn't thinking." She stalked over to the end table, popped off the top, and shook out two tablets.

"Mom, put them away," Kaley said. "I'll take a couple before bed so I can sleep tonight."

"If you're in pain—" Dad started.

"I'm uncomfortable." Kaley started to shake her head before she remembered she was supposed to have a concussion. "There's a big difference."

"Take it easy this afternoon." He squeezed her foot again while Mom returned the pills into the ibuprofen bottle. "I've got my own patient to take care of so I need to get going." He stood up and gathered Mom in his arms.

Theirs wasn't a simple peck. No, they made out like Brad and Amelia used to between classes.

"Oh, Goddess!" Kaley pulled the blanket over her head. "No one wants to see their parents doing that!" One of the cats meowed in agreement.

"Brat," Dad said affectionately. The floor creaked under the rug, and the blanket was jerked from her head. He kissed her forehead. "Be good for your mom. I don't want to explain fireball damage in the living room to your aunts."

"I will."

He kissed Mom again, a briefer one, before he left.

Kaley looked at Mom. A little contrition was needed no matter how stupid everyone blowing up about a skipped study hall was. "Do I need to put the new phone up until the end of the week?"

Mom sighed. "No, I need my phone for work the rest of the afternoon." She narrowed her eyes. "However, if you skip any more classes before the end of the school year, even study hall, you'll lose your phone privileges for a month. Understand?"

"Yes, ma'am."

Mom was trying so hard to be stern Kaley was finding it difficult to keep from laughing. She tried to appear as if she were still very uncomfortable. "Can I ask a favor first?"

"Whatcha need?"

"Can you plug in the power cord for me please?" She held up the bundle of plastic-covered wires.

"Sure." Mom unwound the cord, handed her the end that plugged into the phone, and inserted the converter into the surge-protected power strip beside the couch. "Anything else?" she asked when she straightened.

"No, thank you."

Mom nodded. "I'll be in the dining room working. Yell if you need something."

"Thanks, Mom." Kaley gave her a tremulous smile and prayed Mom would buy it.

Apparently, her ploy worked. After flashing a concerned expression, Mom said, "If you change your mind about the ibuprofen—"

"I'll watch TV while my phone charges, and hopefully, I can take a nap, too."

Mom nodded before she walked toward the doorway to the dining room and disappeared around the corner.

Kaley plugged in her phone and read through the directions pamphlet. According to the manufacturer, it would take approximately an hour for the initial charge to complete. Time for another episode while she waited.

As the show ended, her new phone beeped, indicating it was fully charged. She programmed Kirsten's name and number on the contact page and started texting. She simply couldn't deal with pretending to be injured for the next six weeks. She could not lose her cheerleading position after so many people tried to get her kicked off the squad last month.

Chapter 12

Walking toward the student parking lot, Kirsten wanted to kill Kaley as she stared at the text on her phone. Had Rain screwed with her sister's mind last night? Or was this simply another one of Kaley's hare-brained schemes?

"Hey! Watch where you're walking?"

She jerked her head up and stopped in midstride. Donny stood right in front of her, wearing a devilish grin, but his expression immediately turned more serious.

"Is Kaley okay?" he said. He fell in step beside Kirsten as she continued her path to Mom's sedan.

"Yeah, she's just come up with another of her insane plots." Kirsten glanced at him. "You know, like the ones that usually end up with us getting grounded for a month."

"Maybe she got her clock rung hard enough she forgot she was already grounded," he said.

"Maybe." Kirsten spotted Hope already leaning against Mom's sedan. Hope watched Olivia talking to River in the next row over with an amused look on her face.

Was Olivia flirting with River? As Kirsten and Donny got closer, she could hear the actual conversation.

"But I want to go, too!" Olivia stomped her foot and flipped her braids. She never acted so . . . girly. Especially not around any male.

Kirsten thumbed the key fob to unlock both the car doors and the trunk. Hope tossed in her backpack, except for one notebook and a pen, and immediately claimed the front passenger seat.

"River, you wanna toss your backpack in the trunk?" Kirsten called as she and Donny did that very thing.

"Talk to you later!" River threw his backpack in the open trunk and dived into the back driver-side seat. Olivia stormed off in a royal pout Kirsten thought only Amelia Ryder could have pulled off.

Kirsten slammed the trunk lid shut, and Donny whistled as he examined the multitude of dents and scratches from last night's flying chunks of brick.

"What did your folks say when they saw the car?" he asked.

"Thank Goddess for insurance." Kirsten headed for driver's door and climbed into the sedan. Once Donny was inside the car, she punched the ignition button.

She looked in the rearview mirror at River. "Dude, you have got to tone down the glamour."

"I'm not doing anything," he said angrily.

"Maybe not on purpose," Donny said. "But you're throwing off honey and ozone like a magick-drunk honey bee."

"You're sniffing me?" River sounded outraged.

"We're in an enclosed space," Donny snapped back. "It's hard to miss, even with all the Axe body spray you wear. Not to mention with the three of you together, it smells like a damn bakery in here, and it's making me hungry."

Kirsten couldn't help it. She cracked up, and Hope followed suit.

When Kirsten got herself under control, she said, "Can you two leave the bickering for when I'm not driving?"

"Fine," Donny said equanimously while River muttered, "I didn't start it."

"I'm ending it," Kirsten snapped.

Thankfully, the guys remained silent as she backed out of her parking spot. Her patience threatened to explode since everyone else was leaving the school parking lot at the same time. She was so used to staying for basketball practice or tutoring other students she rarely had to deal with the mass exodus, even on game nights like tonight. Thankfully, everyone remained silent other than Hope humming along with the radio.

Her irritation with the traffic and extra time it took to get to the Painter Building surrendered to anxiety flavored by a touch of guilt as they approached the burned-out husk. At the curb, she pulled in behind a sheriff's department SUV and the white pickup with the fire chief's emblem on the door. After killing the engine, she opened the car door and slid out of the driver seat.

Julia waved from where she was talking with Fire Chief Nicholls. Officer Hatfield, the policeman Mom called Mark at the hospital last night, was with them. Was this a bad sign? In the ER, he and his partner didn't seem to like supernaturals. Kirsten and the other teens approached the three adults.

"What do you want us to do, Deputy Wolford?" Kirsten said.

The fire chief opened his mouth, but Julia held up her hand. "If you don't mind, Chief, I'd like Kirsten and her friends to check out the site before we all compare notes."

He nodded. "Don't taint their impressions. Got it."

"I thought only the Wilson girl was interning with the joint task force," Officer Hatfield said.

Kirsten crossed her arms. "The Wilson girl is standing right here. And both our former sheriff and our current sheriff know what Donny, River, and I can do, which is why Deputy Wolford texted me about meeting her and Chief Nicholls here."

"The sheriff's department isn't running the joint task force by themselves," Officer Hatfield said, coolly.

As Dad would say, time to bring out her inner Spock to make some points without pissing off all the adults.

"I know," Kirsten replied. "Police Chief Hall is the one who's sponsoring my internship, and I understand you're looking out for her interests. But there's a reason Chief Hall and Sheriff Birkheimer had to recruit a witch in high school, and we—" She gestured to indicate her friends. "—all have a vested interest in helping you after my sister was injured by whoever was responsible for the explosion."

Officer Hatfield seemed nonplused by her logical argument, and he didn't say a word.

She turned to Julia and Chief Nicholls. "Any specific spot where you want us to start. Hope and I need to be back at the high school in time for tonight's basketball game so that only gives us roughly three hours."

"Because a high school game is so much more important than any crime that's been committed." Hatfield scowled at her.

"No, it's about honoring our commitments," Kirsten said mildly. "Has Officer Zarnecki recruited you for Humanity Now?"

"What's that supposed to mean?" Hatfield snapped.

"It means Chief Hall's task force won't work if any of the Normal members are anti-supernatural," she replied. "We're here to help." She gestured at her fellow students behind her again. "But if you don't want our assistance, we'll leave so we're not in your way."

Both Julia and the fire chief watched Officer Hatfield with mildly amused expressions on their faces.

Finally, Hatfield said, "I'm not a bigot like Lewis. I just don't see how a bunch of kids can do anything trained professionals can do better."

"I can see it because Patty's right," the fire chief said. "These kids aren't carrying the baggage a coven or pack enforcer would, but they have the same skill sets. The plan is we train 'em in our techniques. But maybe we need to use younger officers on her task-force, too."

Officer Hatfield's ears and cheeks reddened beneath his five o'clock shadow.

"This isn't an issue of admissible evidence," Julia added. "I want them to examine the site. When we compare what we discovered with what they do, we'll know if this taskforce will work."

Kirsten suppressed a shiver. That didn't sound good. It meant her suspicion to why Julia asked her and Donny to come out here was on the nose. They suspected arson, and they suspected a supernatural had performed the deed.

Great. No wonder Hatfield had a broomstick up his ass about her and Donny being here. Why ask your top suspects to help your investigation?

"Donny, I cleared out a spot in the back of my SUV for you to change," Julia said.

"Thanks, Deputy." Donny grinned at Hatfield. "Don't need an indecent exposure charge. I'd hate to miss McKelvey's pizza tonight at the Wilsons after the game."

While Donny followed Julia over to her vehicle, Chief Nicholls stepped closer to Kirsten. "How's your sister doing?"

"Um, the ER released her late last night." Kirsten glanced at Officer Hatfield. "She's rattled and sore as heck from her injuries, but otherwise, okay."

"Good." The fire chief gave a crisp nod. "I see too much of the other side when responding to calls."

Kirsten's stomach clenched at the memory of Kaley bleeding on the pavement. If something more serious had happened to her, Kirsten didn't think she could live with herself when their last words were said in the heat of an argument.

"That's one thing about this town," she smiled at Chief Nicholls. "Everyone watches out for each other like family."

And with a jolt, she realized why Kaley was so peeved about her originally wanting to go somewhere out of state for college. Kaley looked at Kirsten's need to leave Millersburg as abandoning her family.

Julia, who had been guarding the partially closed back doors of her SUV, turned and opened one door wider. Donny leapt down to the cracked pavement and shook himself. His coat was mottled with gray, black, and white except for a touch of red around his snout, ears, and paws. His tail gradually darkened into a black, bushy tip.

He trotted over to Kirsten and looked up expectantly. Normally, Kaley would link with him, and for some weird reason, she was a bit nervous about doing so. She ran her fingers through the fur on his head, and for a split second, she was looking up at her own face from waist level.

After locking her vehicle, Julia rejoined them. "Kirsten, would you mind including everyone in the link so we can all hear Donny?"

"Not at all," she said.

Officer Hatfield literally jumped back. "Wait a minute! No one said anything about letting someone in my head!"

"Dude, chill." River rolled his eyes. "It's a low-level link. It doesn't go beyond talking." He shrugged. "It's just that you'll hear the furry runt in your head since he can't talk when he's on four legs."

Donny's hackles rose, and a low-throated growl came from him. Kirsten bit her lip to keep from laughing at the stream of invectives in her head, but Hope giggled outright.

River gestured nonchalantly at Donny. "Except you don't need a translation for that."

Kirsten held out her left palm. "Everyone who wants in, lay your hand on top of mine."

Julia and Hope did so immediately. After a moment's hesitation, Chief Nicholls laid his hand on top of Hope's. However, Officer Hatfield eyed River with suspicion.

"Why aren't you joining it?" the policeman demanded.

River shook his head. "Lesson number one: fae and witch magick mixes like matter and anti-matter. Either Kirsten runs the link, or I do."

"Or what?" Officer Hatfield said. "You fry our minds?"

Kirsten and River exchanged worried looks.

"No," Kirsten said quietly. "Mixing witch and fae magick results in what happened to the Painter Building."

Chapter 13

Kaley hit the pause button on the remote when the front door opened. Jo entered with a pastry box from her coffee shop.

"How're you feelin', kitten?"

"Better." Kaley grinned. "Did you bring me some goodies?"

"Thought you might need a break from your mom's health food." Jo grinned in return. Unlike Mom's braid, Jo had gone back to wearing her hair in a high ponytail, a style popular when she was Kaley's age. Since the Rainier Outing, she'd also stop dying gray streaks in her mahogany locks. Now, she looked more like Mom's younger sister than the seventy she actually was.

"I heard that," Mom yelled from the dining room.

"Please don't give her a hard time," Kaley begged. "She's letting us get McKelvey's pizza for dinner tonight."

Mom appeared in the doorway between the living room and dining room. "You want to stay for dinner, Jo?"

"What about Kirsten's game?" Jo crossed to the couch and handed the box of goodies to Kaley. She opened the box. Chocolate-frosted Long Johns. Her favorite! She pulled one out and bit into the crème-filled goodie. It wasn't like she was cheerleading this week. Dad may have forgiven her, but Principal Reed sure wouldn't let her one indiscretion go no matter how many boxes of pastries Jo gave him.

"We're picking up the pizzas after the basketball game," Mom answered. "I already called in the order."

Jo gently pushed at Kaley's blanketed feet, and she pulled them out of the way for Jo to sit at the other end of the couch. "Now, what's this about a fae boy at the high school?"

The bite of Long John turned to concrete in Kaley's throat. "It's just—" She swallowed again. "I thought the addendums to the I.C. accords didn't allow fae into Holmes County." She shrugged. "But it turns out River's only half-fae." She took another bite of the doughnut.

"Seelie?" Jo asked.

Kaley shook her head.

Jo's eyes narrowed and her mouth twisted. "A half-Unseelie your age? I don't like the sound of it."

"You remember Cissy Martin's daughter Heather?" Mom said.

"Of course." Jo looked over at Mom. "Cissy said they'd made up after her heart attack, and Heather was moving back here. This is Heather's kid?"

Kaley swallowed. The filled doughnut tasted like sawdust. She placed the half-eaten Long John back in the box. "I'm sorry. I panicked when I texted you. I talked to River for a while yesterday afternoon. He's actually pretty nice."

Jo's left eyebrow rose. "And why were you talking to him yesterday?"

"Because Kirsten and Donny were pretty nasty to the poor guy." Kaley waved her hands, or she tried to. Thankfully, the sling didn't let her give everything away. "It's not his fault his mom had a one-night stand with a fae guy."

"Sweetheart, when it comes to fae, we have to look beyond the obvious." Mom shook her head, a sad expression on her face. "You can't accept anything River says or does at face value."

A breeze wafted through the living room in reaction to Kaley's emotions, ruffling the college paperwork on the end table she had been filling out over the weekend. With extreme effort, she stilled the air.

"You guys are just like Kirsten," she bit out. "What happened to innocent until proven guilty?"

Jo reached over and grasped Kaley's left hand. "Girl, did you know he laid a spell on you?"

Oh, Goddess! So much for her plan to explain why she was fine. Kaley clutched her blanket and licked her lips. "Yes, I know, and he did it with my permission."

"You foolish brat!" Jo jumped up from the couch. "Do you have a death wish?"

Kaley sat up, yanked off her sling, and frantically waved her hands. "Wait! It's not what you think."

"What do you mean Kaley Ophelia Wilson?" Mom snapped.

Crap. The middle name meant her grounding had just been extended. Consigned to facing the consequences, Kaley lowered her arms and clutched her blanket. "River felt my pain from across town, and he healed me last night. He wanted to help me. Please don't be mad at him for that."

Jo narrowed her eyes. "He healed you from that far away?"

"No." Kaley picked at the stray cat hairs on her blanket. "He came over because he was worried about me."

"And how did he know where we live?" Mom asked.

"He followed my pain," Kaley said. Her eyes started to burn. "The ibuprofen was barely making a dent. And it was a good thing he came. I was bleeding in my brain—"

"Wait a minute," Mom barked. "How did he get into the house?"

"Oh, sweet Goddess," Jo swore. "Please tell me you didn't let him in."

Their attitude was starting to get on Kaley's nerves, but she wasn't about to throw Kirsten under the bus, too. "Yes, I invited him in because I was afraid of him falling out of the tree. He was trying to help! I don't get why you're making such a big deal about this!"

Mom wiped her hands down her face. "Kirsten was supposed to be watching you last night."

"She was," Kaley said. "But she was in the bathroom when he showed up. She didn't like the idea of River healing me, but I told her I had nothing to lose at that point. He saved my life, Mom. The ER docs missed the bleeding in my brain."

"You don't understand how dangerous the fae are, Kaley," Jo said. Her voice was low and ugly. Her anger flowed in palpable waves of heat. Sweat prickled along Kaley's forehead.

"You both say the same thing about werecoyotes," she said, looking from her aunt to her mom and back. "Only Chad Fryer and part of the Killbuck pack sided with the Winter Queen's people during the Battle of Millersburg, but you both accept me and Kirsten being friends with Donny." She lifted her chin. "River's mom got knocked up by one of those fae, whether by her choice or because she was bespelled. Neither of which matters because it still wasn't River's fault any more than it is Donny's fault who his father was."

Kaley could hear her voice rising, but she couldn't seem to stop herself. "The reason I hid the healing from you is because I knew this is exactly how both of you would react! Like a couple of Normals afraid of their own damn shadows!"

She turned back to Mom. "Since I'm grounded for lying and letting a male into the house after hours, I'll go upstairs to my room so I don't have to hear any more of your racist bullshit."

Kaley flung back the blanket and stood. She handed the new phone to Mom. "The passcode is six-zero-zero-seven since you'll want to check to see if I talked to him this afternoon." She took two steps toward the stairs before she whirled around to face Mom again. "By the way, River was a perfect gentleman. He left as soon as he completed the healing." She brushed past Jo and ran up the stairs.

It was hard to resist the urge to slam her door shut, but somehow, Kaley managed. She flung herself on the unmade bed. How did everything go so wrong this week?

An irritated cat meowed in the upstairs hall. It was followed by a gold paw reaching under her bedroom door.

"You scratch the hardwood, and you know Mom will skin you alive," Kaley murmured.

The paw withdrew, and she rolled off the bed and crossed to the door. When she opened it, Penn strolled in like he owned the place. He leapt up on her bed and looked over his shoulder as if to say, "Are you coming?"

Kaley closed the door again and returned to her bed. Penn climbed into her lap. He stretched to rub his cheek against hers.

"You would have told me if River was a bad person, wouldn't you?"

Penn meowed before he climbed off her lap and curled up next to her pillow. She lay down next to him and stroked his soft gold fur.

How the hell had she managed to screw up her life this much in less than a week? And how the hell did she fix it?

Chapter 14

Officer Hatfield, Fire Chief Nicholls, and Julia stared at River, and Kirsten couldn't blame them. Heck, she didn't need a telepathic link to know she'd thought the very same things that were obviously going through their minds right now.

"No witch or fae in their right mind starts throwing magick at each other," Julia said.

"And how do we know any of these kids are in their right minds?" Hatfield replied. "Maybe that's how her sister really go hurt." He pointed his chin in Kirsten's direction. "Maybe these two were tossing spells at each other inside the Painter Building, and things got out of hand."

"We already saw the security video from inside the auto parts store, Mark," Julia said.

"Maybe she—" Officer Hatfield started.

"Either join us, or quit yer bitchin' and let us get to work, Mark Hatfield," Hope said. "Or do I need to tell Aunt Sally how yer actin'?"

Officer Hatfield's mouth dropped open. It took him a couple of tries before he finally said, "Why are you dragging our families into this, Hope?"

Sweet Goddess! Kirsten managed not to laugh. She'd totally forgotten Hope's Aunt Sally had eloped to Vegas with Mark Hatfield's brother Malcolm last Valentine's Day. It was the second marriage for both of them, and the elopement had been the talk of this very conservative town. From the way Julia snorted, she hadn't forgotten either.

"I'm not the one acting like a douche about free help," Hope bit back. "And I'm not chicken either."

Scowling at Hope, Officer Hatfield laid his palm on the stack of hands. "If anything happens to me, I'm blaming you, Hope Stillwell."

Kirsten placed her right palm on top of Officer Hatfield's rough skin and concentrated. Once again, she felt the dissonance of River's magick against hers, but he kept himself in check.

Can you hear me now? Donny mimicked the ancient phone commercial.

"Yep." Julia grinned. "Damn, I miss my stepbrothers sometimes." She turned serious. "Donny, do a perimeter sweep around the building, then work your way inside. Don't go past anyplace with tape. We don't have a healer in town."

A touch of guilt settled in the back of Kirsten's mind, but River's secret wasn't hers to share.

He shaded his eyes against the setting sun as he examined the remnants of the structure. "Shouldn't we be wearing hardhats?"

"I've got a couple in my truck if you want them," Chief Nicholls said. "But don't go crawling under anything or on top debris. This is an off-the-record looksee by you guys based on Deputy Wolford's say so."

"Yes, sir." Kirsten nodded before she turned Hope. "Take notes, but whatever you do, don't go inside that building."

"Got it, boss." Hope held up her notebook and pen.

The fire chief retrieved two fire department helmets for Kirsten and River. Donny trotted off towards the back of the ruined building with Julia jogging behind him. Kirsten and the rest headed for what had been the main entrance.

The explosion had blasted out the glass in the doors and windows. Whatever jagged pieces that were left had been knocked out by the firefighters before they pulled hoses inside to drench the remaining embers of the building.

Kirsten stepped inside of the charred framework of the main doors. Part of the roof had collapsed at the rear of the building as had a good chunk of the southern wall. The cave-in had brought down parts of the second and third floors. Solid timbers at the front showed charring, but they looked stable.

"Let me go first," she said quietly to River. She half-expected him to argue, but he remained silent and merely nodded.

Kirsten closed her eyes and extended her senses. Magick permeated the area, but it didn't have only the rasp of fae. She connected with the water from the hydrants that had coated the ashes and soot-stained brick and felt her way toward the middle of the first floor. Witch earth magick rested among shards of a different type of power scattered through the ruin. More of a memory than real power. Still, she carefully withdrew.

She opened her eyes and nodded to River.

He sucked in a deep breath and closed his eyes before he slowly released the air from his lungs. His magick prickled her skin.

If witch magick was drawn as a sine wave, fae magick would be a cosine wave, which was part of the reason they canceled out each other violently.

When his eyes opened, the blue irises sparked with his anger. "I wasn't here last night," he bit out.

"But it's definitely the remains of fae magick, right?" Kirsten looked up at him.

"And witch magick," he snapped.

"Yeah, I know." She crossed her arms. "I was really hoping we were wrong about this."

"You two saying someone set off one of your anti-matter bombs in here?" Chief Nicholls asked.

"Yes, but the witch magick is definitely earth magic," she said to the chief. She turned back to River. "Can you tell the difference between Unseelie and Seelie magick?"

He nodded. "It's definitely Unseelie." He ran a hand through his white-blond locks, making them stand on end. "I went back to the hotel after I talked to Kaley after school."

Donny slipped past the group without a word. His nose worked overtime as he prowled through the ruins he was allowed to access. Julia joined them.

"Did anyone see you, River?" the deputy asked gently.

He shook his head. "I used my keycard to go through one of the side exits since we're at that end of the hallway."

"You're at the Holiday Inn, right?" Julia asked. She had her own notepad out and scribbled in it.

"Yes." His shoulders sagged. "But Mom didn't get back to our room until seven. Are you going to arrest me?"

"No," Officer Hatfield said. "We'll check the keycard access and the security footage. Luckily, the Holiday Inn opened recently and has updated measures. But don't leave town until we clear you."

Wow. Kirsten had to give the policeman credit for changing his attitude after last night. Or maybe it was Hope's threat of causing trouble with their families. Either way, it would make things easier.

"You said the witch magick was earth magick," Chief Nicholls said. "What do you mean by that?"

Kirsten pulled her pentacle from beneath her sweatshirt. "The five points of the star represent the five elements: earth, water, fire, air, and spirit. Most of us are born with an affinity towards one. Mine's water. The witch spell in here was made by someone who leans toward earth magick."

"How can you tell the difference?" Officer Hatfield asked.

Kirsten shrugged. "How do you tell the difference between water cupped in one hand and field soil in the other?"

"Which of you gals in town has this affinity to earth?" Officer Hatfield seemed genuinely curious.

Kirsten didn't like being a narc, but this was serious. "The only person I know is Tina Eisler, but she's not a full-blooded witch. Her power is limited to an awesome garden and moving pens across a table."

This gets better. Donny trotted up to them. *I'm not scenting either ginger or honey anywhere around here. Just apple.*

"What does that mean?" Officer Hatfield said.

Julia's face turned red, and her eyes have off a hard glint. "He means it was a Normal who set off the explosion."

Chapter 15

Someone knocked on her bedroom door. Kaley raised her head and felt the presence of Jo.

"What do you want?" Kaley yelled.

Jo opened the door. "Maybe I deserve that. For some reason, I thought you might have cooled down enough to talk."

Teller jumped to his paws and hissed at Jo.

Kaley sat up on her bed. "I wasn't the one throwing accusations around downstairs."

"You're right." Jo's shoulders slumped. "Which is why I wanted to talk to you."

"Why? You've already made up your mind without even meeting River." Kaley dropped back on the mattress and flung her right arm over her eyes, hoping Jo would take the hint.

"And you're acting like a brat, which is exactly why I'm watching you tonight," Jo snapped.

"Maybe I'm overreacting like every other woman in our family." Kaley lifted her right arm. "You think Kirsten and I don't know exactly what Aunt Ophelia says about Dad behind his back?"

Jo's cheeks turned a deep rose color, and she cleared her throat. "This isn't about my sister."

Kaley sat up. "No, it's about the entire coven. None of them would give Mom the time of day until we started showing our abilities. Once they were assured we were 'real' witches, then the other kids of the coven would talk to us. Not before. And Kirsten and I know damn well where that attitude comes from. How can we expect the Normals to fully accept the supernaturals when we can't accept each other, much less them?"

Jo looked up at the ceiling for a moment. "You're right." She sighed and looked down at Kaley. "I was angry your parents encouraged your sister to join the law enforcement task force Patty Hall is putting together. I thought it was a way for the Normals to turn a witch into a witch hunter. But maybe we did that all by ourselves."

"Dad's the real reason you moved down to Millersburg, isn't it?"

Jo chuckled. "Just a little bit. However, I really did want to get away from my jerk of an ex-husband. It's amazing how you can be with someone for twenty-five years and not really know them."

"Tell me about it," Kaley grumbled.

Jo pulled a phone out of her pocket. One that wasn't hers. "Speaking of family, Kirsten's been texting you. She wants you to do some research about witch and fae magicks interacting. She suspects someone's either experimenting or trying to set up the supernaturals to make them look bad."

"What?" Kaley accepted her new phone and scrolled through all the messages her twin had left since the argument with Mom and Jo this afternoon. It wasn't just Kirsten blowing up her phone. Donny and River had, too, about the investigation into the explosion at the Painter Building. Other friends checked in to see how she was doing and asked when she'd be back at school. Josh left a sweet message, asking her to a movie once she was feeling better.

She scrolled back to Kirsten's text stream and skimmed the issues again before she looked up at Jo. "I'm going to ask you something, Aunt Jo, and I really need you to be honest with me. How suicidal were the Unseelie during the Battle of Millersburg?"

"Suicidal?"

"Were they slinging spells?"

Jo blinked. "No, they weren't. But after what Anne Levy and Leslie Warner did to some of them and the Amish coming after them with steel farm tools, I don't think any of the Unseelie were thinking straight."

"Were you or Mom throwing spells that night?"

Jo nodded. "I was. Your mother was pregnant with you two."

She smiled. "It took a vampire and the Amish elders to talk her out of coming with us. She wasn't listening to anyone, even your father, that night."

"So, none of the fae raised wards or threw offensive spells?"

"Nope. I threw first, so they didn't dare use magick. They stuck to conventional weapons that night."

"Let me get a shower and get dressed." Kaley looked at her phone again. "I think someone's trying to set up the Winter Court, but the question is who and why."

Jo shook her head as Kaley climbed out of bed and shed her bathrobe. "The only people with a direct grievance against the fae are those who lost family members. I can't see Rose or any of the Amish seeking revenge. And the Killbuck pack would have done something stupid long before now if they wanted to retaliate."

Kaley grabbed jeans and a West Holmes sweatshirt from her dresser and tossed them on the bed. Jo and Mom had to have read Kirsten's texts. "Then why did Donny only pick up human scents in and around the Painter Building, but Kirsten and River picked up both fae and witch magick residue?"

"Because no one in the fire department is a supernatural." Jo crossed her arms. "Not to mention the water from the fire hoses would have washed away most scents."

"Both you and Tina sell charms." Kaley tossed her nightgown on the bed.

"And Kirsten only detected earth magick," Jo shot back.

"So, are we back to blaming Tina for every magical thing that goes wrong in town?" Kaley threw her hands in the air. "Because you and Mom bound Noah and Mila's powers when we discovered they were dreamwalkers."

"Can we stop arguing long enough for you to get your shower?" Jo said dryly. "It's bad enough I'm missing tonight's basketball game."

Kaley rolled her eyes and stalked out of her bedroom.

Once Kaley was dressed and clipped her damp hair out of her face, she examined herself in her vanity's mirror. Dark circles marred the skin under her eyes, but her fatigue was due to River's healing spell. Those things exhausted both the caster and the recipient. However, she didn't miss last night's broken shoulder blade or her awful headache. How much of the headache was the concussion and how much was from the blood filling her cranium? Something deep inside her knew River hadn't been lying when he said her injury was more severe than what the Normal doctors believed.

She jogged back down the stairs. Jo sat on the couch. The weird part was Penn and Teller sitting in front of the dark TV screen and staring at Jo.

"Stop it, you two," Kaley snapped. "You're both worse than Amelia Ryder about grudges."

Penn and Teller turned their heads in unison to look at Kaley. Penn snorted and butted his brother with his head hard enough to knock Teller over before he stalked into the dining room. Teller glared at Kaley as if the whole thing was her fault before he ran after his brother.

Jo shook her head. "Sometimes, I swear those two act just like your Grandma Charlie."

Kaley approached the couch, but she couldn't bring herself to sit down. Instead, she crossed her arms. "Did Mom call the healer from Cleveland and cancel?"

Jo nodded. "Not that I think any of the Cleveland healers were going to come down here any time soon."

"What did she tell them?" Kaley asked.

"That Kirsten was keeping you comfortable." Jo shrugged.

"So, she lied to the coven?" Kaley dropped her arms and perched gingerly on the other end of the couch. "Does that mean she listened to me when I said River actually saved my life last night?"

"Let's just say we're both reserving judgment when it comes to River Martin." Jo breathed deeply and let the air out in a rush. "It would have caused more problems if Rachel told them a half-fae was here in Millersburg."

"You mean she was afraid the news would start another supernatural war?" Kaley twisted her fingers together.

"Exactly," Jo admitted.

"Holding on to these ancient blood feuds is ridiculous," Kaley murmured. "Especially now that the Normals know about us. By the way, I overheard Mom talking on the phone earlier. She said that one of the cops questioning me last night was a member of Humanity Now. Has it occurred to either of you there may be someone else with a motive to cause trouble for us?"

Jo blinked and stared at her oddly. "But where would they get access to fae magick?"

Damn, everything kept pointing back to River. How the heck would Kaley find a way to prove his innocence?

Chapter 16

Kirsten stared at the werecoyote. "Are you sure you only detect Normals?"

Yep. He gave a very human nod. *You and Honey Boy here are the only supernaturals, and you both just walked onto the property. If another fae or witch were here, I would have picked up their trail when they left.*

"Don't call me Honey Boy," River snapped.

Then don't smell like it, Donny shot back.

"Did you guys find any bodies?" Kirsten looked at the three adults.

All three of them shook their heads.

"This reaction between the two different types of magick." Chief Nicholls waved at the remnants of the Painter Building. "What would it have done to the bodies?"

Kirsten hugged herself. Magick interaction explained the low-level headache she'd had since last night. She had attributed it to the pressure wave of the blast. It also explained why the explosion knocked Kaley on her ass despite throwing up a ward.

"There would be bodies," Kirsten said. "They may be in pieces from the blast and charred from the fire, but there would have been bodies."

Maybe not, Donny said. *You're assuming two casters were in here tossing spells. We're the first supernaturals to step on this property for at least a week.*

"You can only smell back that far?" Officer Hatfield said.

No. There was a long pause.

Kirsten smashed her own giggle at Donny's effort not to call the policeman obscene names.

It rained last Thursday. Water washes away some of the scent, but not all of it. Time does the rest, Donny continued. *That's why Deputy Wolford wanted me to check the perimeter first, well outside of the fire department's splash zone.*

"We already know no one entered or left via the front of the Painter Building thanks to the security cameras at the auto supply store across the street and the bank on the corner." Julia pointed at the two businesses.

For the first time, Hope spoke up. "What if I carried something that contained a spell, could I activate it?"

"Whoever laid the spell on the object would have to create a trigger for the Normal," River said.

"Not necessarily," Kirsten interjected. "Jo does charms for people all the time. Those are already active."

"But if the person brought two active charms of the two different magicks in close proximity, that's a great way to commit suicide" River argued.

"If they had a witch charm and a fae charm with the same trigger, couldn't they have some kind of delay switch?" Hope looked at Kirsten and River in turn.

Kirsten stared up at River. He stared back.

"That would be awfully risky," she murmured.

He spread his hands. "I have no idea. I was lucky one of my teachers in Indianapolis was half-fae, but he didn't know a whole lot about magick, and most of it was trial and error on both of our parts."

"Wait a minute," Officer Hatfield said. "The fae can have babies with humans?"

"Yes," Kirsten said. "But it's usually just Normals."

"And they send those kids out into the world with no clue of how to manage their powers and no way to learn?" Hatfield continued.

Yep. Donny smiled a doggie grin. *The weres don't look so bad now, do they?*

"Why would any woman do that?" Hatfield looked horrified.

However, River's face turned beet red. "What exactly are you trying to insinuate about my mom, Officer?"

"It's not just Normal women," Kirsten said. "It can happen with Normal men, too."

"Why?" Julia asked, but she was merely curious.

Same reason everybody else does it, Donny said. *They want to get laid.* He chuckled. *Though the fae ladies mainly want to piss off their husbands.*

"Folks, let's focus on the problem at hand," Chief Nicholls interjected before more arguing could get started. "Let's disregard the risk for the moment. Does Hope's theory have merit?"

Kirsten frowned. Kaley said she saw a light, possibly a flame, inside the building prior to the explosion. "Yes, but have you ruled out any other possibilities?"

"We're waiting on the lab tests to confirm everything." Chief Nicholls scrunched his face. "But we couldn't find anything like an accelerant. No bomb fragments." He gestured toward the back. "It didn't start anywhere near the natural gas line coming into the building, the gas company turned off the gas after the building was abandoned, and the street cut-off hasn't been touched in decades. I had the gas people come out this morning. No leaks. It's like the damn explosion and fire started in the middle of the first-floor front room near absolutely nothing."

Kirsten's phone alarm beeped. She pulled it out of her jeans pocket and turned off the alarm. "Hope and I have to get back to the high school."

I want to stay and make another sweep, Donny protested.

"How can we hear him if you leave?" Officer Hatfield protested. For someone who acted adverse to magick when Kirsten and her carload arrived, he was all for it now.

"I can do the link when Kirsten leaves, but my car is still at the high school," River said.

So's mine, Donny added.

"I'll drop you boys off at West Holmes after we're done," Julia offered.

Once everything was settled, and River retrieved the guys' backpacks from the trunk, Kirsten and Hope hopped into Mom's car. As Kirsten pulled out into traffic, Hope asked, "Can we stop at Burger King on the way? I need a little something before the game."

"That was my plan," Kirsten said.

They were halfway to the fast-food restaurant when Hope asked, "Are you okay?"

"Yeah, why?"

"You were basically narcing on your own people back there." Hope sighed. "I've seen the news. There's been some backlash against supernaturals in the big cities."

Kirsten glanced at Hope. She was probably the closest friend Kirsten had in this town outside of her sister, but she and Kaley hadn't been that close lately. Kaley wasn't happy about Kirsten planning to attend college outside of Ohio. "Is that why you suggested it may have been a Normal who set off the explosion?"

"No, I mentioned it because it seemed to be the logical conclusion." Hope drummed her fingers against her right knee. "Officer Hatfield's absolutely sure the culprit is supernatural, Deputy Wolford is sure it isn't, and Chief Nicholls is just confused because he's never seen a fire like this before."

"Do you think it was arson?" Kirsten asked as she hit the turn signal for the hamburger place's driveway.

Hope stopped drumming her fingers. "Don't know. It could be no different than leaving matches or a lighter where your little kid can reach them."

Kirsten grimaced. Hope sounded like the narrator in the program they'd watched in current events class two years ago. The one about the pros and cons of everybody knowing about and having access to magick. The program had taken the conjecture to the worst conclusion—that nations would weaponize supernatural folks against each other.

"Then we need to find this idiot and stop them," Kirsten muttered. "Before something worse happens than my twin sister's head hitting concrete."

Kirsten glanced up in the stands while the two basketball teams warmed up on the court. She didn't expect Kaley to attend, but Josh Fairbanks must have. He sat beside Mom and Dad at the top benches. Dad always sat at the top. He claimed he didn't want to block anyone's view because of his height.

Even more surprising, Donny and River sat on the other side of her parents. Well, Mom had agreed to River coming over for a late dinner tonight.

Olivia tossed the ball to Kirsten and she took the three steps for an easy layup and missed.

Again.

The ball pinged off the backboard into Hope's hands. "What's wrong with you? You haven't hit a practice shot yet."

Heat flooded Kirsten's face. "Just been a crazy week." She jogged to the back of the rebound line. Dang, she needed to get her crap together. Indian Valley wasn't going to be a pushover. Not this year anyway.

She glanced behind her. Tacy Summers, the Braves' best player, tossed in another three-pointer like she was frickin' LeBron. Tacy high-fived another player when she caught sight of Kirsten staring at her.

Tacy grinned and pointed at herself, then Kirsten. Last, Tacy flashed all her right fingers, with her matching Braves red polish on her nails, twice. So, that was the bet between them. Tacy planned to outscore Kirsten by ten.

Kirsten rolled her eyes, shook her head, and turned back to the rebound line.

Only to find Coach Park in front of her. "Don't let Summers get into your head, Wilson."

Kirsten lifted her chin. "I won't, Coach."

Coach Park leaned closer and whispered, "And you might want to evict all the other people living up there rent free while you're at it." She turned and walked back toward the West Holmes' bench.

Kirsten sucked in a deep breath and released it. The coach was right. She was letting all the crap with Kaley, her suspicions of River, and her worry over the arson take over her brain space.

She nabbed the basketball as Olivia's shot fell through the net and fired it to Hope. The horn sounded as Hope launched into a perfect layup.

The team gathered the practice balls and handed them to the team manager who placed them on the rolling rack. Coach Park snapped her fingers for silence, and the team gathered around her and settled down.

"This is the second game of the year," Coach said. "You did great in our season opener on Monday, but don't take that victory for granted. Don't hog the ball, and look for opportunities." She seemed to eye Kirsten for more than a second. "Now, let's get out there and hustle!"

Everyone joined hands in the circle. "Go-o-o-o Knights!"

As their tallest player, Hope lined up for the tip-off. What most competitors learned the hard way was the blonde could also jump, too. The referee blew his whistle and toss the basketball straight up. Hope neatly flicked the ball into Olivia's hands.

And the game was on.

Kirsten toweled the sweat from her face. Fourth quarter. Five seconds to go on the clock. Not only were they tied with Indian Valley, she and Tacy were tied for total points scored. Coach Park called her standard end-of-the-game play.

"I see that smirk Kirsten Wilson," Olivia hissed. "Get yer pride out of the way."

Irritation wiggled in Kirsten's brain, but dang, Olivia was right. Tacy had been literally skin-to-skin with Kirsten all night. "Got it, boss lady."

Olivia took the ball from the ref at the sideline, and he blew the whistle to start the clock. She bounced it to Kirsten. As Olivia expected, Tacy was in Kirsten's face. She whirled as if to break for the basket.

Instead, Kirsten continued the spin and passed the ball to Hope. In desperation, the other four Indian Valley girls swarmed the Knights' center. She ducked and did a short bounce-pass between the legs of one of the Braves' players. Olivia snatched the ball and sprang up for the shot.

Someone screamed in the stands. Kirsten looked up. Dad and Donny were crouched over Josh on the top step of the spectator stands, and there was blood.

A lot of blood smeared on the gymnasium wall.

Her heart tried to jump out of her throat at the same time the horn blasted announcing the end of the game.

Chapter 17

Kaley sat at the dining room table and nibbled on a cheesecake Danish from Jo's box of treats while the pair of them researched the possible causes of the explosion based on what Kirsten, Donny, and River picked up in and around the Painter Building this afternoon. When Kaley couldn't find anything in Mom's Book of Shadows about magick interaction other than the standard warnings against mixing witch and fae energies, she switched to Grandma Charlie's. Jo had brought her own Book of Shadows and paged through it slowly reading each entry.

"I need more tea." Jo pushed to her feet. "Would you like some?"

"No, thanks." Kaley looked up from Grandma Charlie's Book of Shadows. "What if there's nothing here because no one's ever tried to figure out how to safely use witch and fae magicks together?"

Jo set the kettle on the burner and turned around with a frown on her face. "Actually, the witches and half-fae on the West Coast have been experimenting with that very thing."

"They have?" Kaley tilted her head. "Why aren't we doing this?"

"Because of the danger," Jo said wryly. "Not to mention, none of the covens on this side of the Mississippi trust the Unseelie."

"So, the West Coast covens trust the Seelie halflings?" Kaley rose to grab another pop from the refrigerator.

Jo frowned before she pulled out her phone. "Last I heard, Master St. James had several Unseelie halflings working for him, not Seelie. It's still early in Los Angeles. Let me ask Anne before I whack a hornet's nest."

She tapped her screen before she raised her phone to her ear. "Hi, Anne. It's Jo Bice. My niece Kaley is here. Do you mind if I put you on speaker phone?" She lowered the phone and tapped the screen again.

"Hello, Kaley," Anne Levy-Fitzgerald said. "How are your parents?"

"They're doing fine." Even though Kaley had known Mary's great-great-aunt since she was little, Anne intimidated the heck out of her. The former Amish woman may be tiny and demure, but she'd also been the head of personal security for Master St. James's predecessor of the Western U.S. Vampire Coven before she took the cure for the V-virus. Even Aunt Jo had a healthy respect for the former vampire and her fighting skills.

"I take it there's been an incident for which you need an independent opinion, Jo," Anne said.

The kettle's piercing whistle overpowered Jo's response. She grabbed a potholder and moved the kettle to an unlit burner before she turned off the one she'd been using.

Anne chuckled. "While it's nice to know some people can make a proper cup of tea, I'm certainly glad I've been reduced to Normal hearing."

"Why don't you tell Anne what happened yesterday, and what Kirsten and Julia found this afternoon?" Jo handed Kaley her phone before she turned back to the cupboard for another tea bag.

Kaley quickly laid out what she saw at the Painter Building before the explosion. She ended up forwarding the afternoon texts from Kirsten and Donny to Anne.

"Is this River another witch?" the former enforcer asked.

"No, he's half-fae himself," Kaley admitted. "I think his mom may have been knocked up by one of the Unseelie with Duke Hoarancill shortly before the Battle of Millersburg, but he said he has no idea who his biological father is."

"Have you confirmed the rest of his story independently?" Anne asked.

Irritation buzzed underneath Kaley's skin. "I know you all have a past with the Unseelie, but that doesn't automatically make River a liar."

"I would ask the same if he were a were, witch, or vampire," Anne said gently. "However, two of Hoarancill's offspring are members of the St. James Coven. I can ask them in regards to River's past if you can give me his mother's name."

"Wait a minute," Jo interjected. "Master St, James accepted two Unseelie into his ranks after what they tried to do to his wife?"

"Stanley joined our coven a century before the current master." Anne sighed. "The surviving fae with Hoarancill the night of the battle were exiled from their Court. The master decided it would be best to offer them a place with us to prevent anymore mischief."

From the look on Jo's face, Anne definitely understated the situation.

"River's mom is Heather Martin," Jo said. "Heather's mother is Cissy Martin who owns The Hair and Now salon."

"Deputy Julia Wolford already ran a background check on River," Kaley said. "That's the only way she would have agreed to letting him help Kirsten and Donny this afternoon."

"Julia knows both Normal and supernatural investigation techniques," Anne said. "And her father Thaddeus has also worked with the coven's fae members in Las Vegas."

"Could you double-check with your fae members about River for me?" Jo pleaded.

"Of course." Anne sounded amused.

"Assuming I or the fae with your coven can prove River's innocence, is there a way to use fae and witch magicks without blowing up everything around us?" Kaley drawled.

"Yes," Anne said. "But it sounds like someone deliberately mixed them with the intent to destroy from the damage to the Painter Building you described and the injuries you sustained."

"What are you planning, Kaley Ophelia?" The warning in Aunt Jo's voice was quite plain.

"I'm not planning anything," Kaley retorted. "We need to know how to defuse a magick bomb before this idiot tries to blow up something besides an empty building."

"Jo, may I contact people within our coven who are more knowledgeable about different magicks and call you later tonight or tomorrow morning?" Anne asked. "I believe Kaley is correct to assume your bomber will try again."

"That would be fine." Jo exhaled heavily. "Thank you for your help, Anne. I really appreciate it."

Anne laughed softly. "Part of me still considers Holmes County as home, so I'm happy to assist. I will text you when I know something."

"No, please call me no matter how late it is on our side of the country," Jo insisted. "If this is triggering your enforcer instincts, then we need to find the culprit now." She and her friend said their goodbyes before Jo ended the call and turned to Kaley. "I'm sorry for doubting you, Kaley."

"But not for assuming River is the bad guy?"

"Don't push it, young lady." Jo scowled at her. "You're only seventeen. You haven't—"

"Seen what you've been through," Kaley said. "But trust between the different supernaturals needs to start somewhere if we want any actual shot of peace on this side of the Mississippi, not the brittle cold war stalemate we've got."

Jo blinked. "I apologize for underestimating you, sweetie. You're right."

While Jo's admission felt good, Kaley didn't have the slightest clue of how she was going to pull off such a crazy feat.

Chapter 18

Kirsten shoved past Tacy and raced up the bleacher stairs. "Check him for a hex charm!"

Donny rifled through Josh's pockets while Dad tried to keep Josh from choking on the blood pouring from his mouth.

"Here!" Donny tossed something shiny at Kirsten.

She snagged the damp, silver object. Alien magick poked at her. It was one of the quartz and silver necklaces Tina sold through Nana's Gift Shop, but it was the harsh buzz of the tiny silver Celtic knot charm between the violet beads that made her heart seize. And the whole damn thing was wet from Josh's sweat.

"Mom!"

Kirsten turned and raced down the steps, pushing people out of the way. She tore across the court. Her high-tops screeched as she rounded the corner. She raced down the hallway. Pounding foot-steps came from behind her. She hit the door and plunged outside.

And immediately started shivering when the frigid November wind hit her sweaty body. Mom slid to a stop next to her.

"Throw it!" Mom yelled.

Kirsten took a couple of steps and launched the necklace like it was a shotput. The wind seemed to catch the silver and quartz beads and took it higher. Mom three fireballs in rapid succession.

They both dove for the dormant grass. Mom landed on top of Kirsten and raised a ward around them. However, the shield didn't stop the explosion from rattling the ground and Kirsten's teeth.

"Good throw," Mom murmured before she dropped her ward and rolled off Kirsten.

The sweet odor of burning grass tickled Kirsten's nose. She looked up. A huge crater smoked in the slope down to the bus depot. Thank Goddess, there was plenty of empty space, and no one was hurt by the magickal interaction.

Her blood chilled at the thought of the improvised magickal explosive device going off in the gymnasium. It could have killed everyone at the girls' basketball game.

She stood and gave Mom a hand up before she summoned the moisture from the dew-laden ground to extinguish the smoldering section of schoolyard.

In the distance, sirens wailed. Dad or Donny must have called 9-1-1 for Josh.

Kirsten was still trying to catch her breath and wishing her ears would stop ringing when Principal Reed, the West Holmes athletic director, and a ton of parents charged out of the same door she and Mom had burst through moments ago. All of them stared at the huge black hole on the school grounds.

Well, all of them except Principal Reed.

"Now, we know who set off the bomb in the Painter Building," he roared.

Before Kirsten could react to his accusations, Mom marched over to him until they were nose-to-nose. "You'd better watch what you say next, Lester Reed. I'm done with you singling out my girls and accusing them of everything under the sun."

"Stop it!" Kirsten yelled. "Both of you!"

To her surprise, all of the adults abruptly went silent, including Sergeant Higgins and Officer Mundy of the Millersburg Police Department who were providing tonight's security. They all stared at her.

"Someone planted a hex on Josh Fairbanks." Kirsten waved at the crater. "A hex powerful enough it could have killed everyone at tonight's game. So, stop squawking at each other, and let law enforcement do their jobs."

She had to yell the last part over the wailing sirens as two firetrucks, an ambulance, and three law enforcement vehicles roared up the driveway to a halt in front of the high school's main entrance. Officer Mundy ran over to the firetrucks.

"Over here, chief!" he shouted, waving his arms to get Chief Nicholls' attention. Kirsten couldn't hear what he said to the chief, but Nicholls began bellowing orders to his people. One set of firefighters raced around, dragging out hoses towards the crater. The other set went inside the high school with the EMTs.

There was a weird sound underneath the shouts of the first responders and the growl of the engines. It took Kirsten a few seconds to realize it was her own teeth chattering. With her adrenaline rush fading, her body decided to point out how cold it was outside.

"S-s-sergeant H-higgins, I need to go to the locker room and grab my stuff," she said. "I-it's a little cold out here for just my uniform."

The police officer nodded. "Just need a statement from you before you leave."

She turned to re-enter the school, and Principal Reed stepped in front of her.

"No, you're not going anywhere," he snarled. "You should be in handcuffs!"

"Oh, for the love of—" The athletic director bit off whatever blasphemy he was about to utter because of the number of parents surrounding him. "Kirsten, go change your clothes. Lester—" He glanced at Mom. "Let's go to your office. Sarge, let the chiefs and Sheriff Birkheimer know where we are."

Kirsten stepped around Principal Reed and headed for the door to the gym's back hallway.

Behind her, Mom said, "Sergeant, let me go in and grab my coat, too. I'll be right back to give you my own statement."

Silently, Mom said, *Are you okay, sweetie?*

Yeah, just please tell me we're still getting McKelvey's pizza tonight. I don't know how much more crap I can handle after the last two days.

Chapter 19

Thankfully, Penn waited until Jo had ended her call with the former vampire enforcer before he jumped up on Kaley's chair and started yowling for his supper. Teller was nowhere to be seen.

Kaley set her can of pop on the table and propped her fists on her hips while she glared at the golden tabby. "You are the most spoiled cat on this side of the Mississippi."

Penn yowled even more insistently. His piteous cries could easily be translated into "I'm starving" in any human language.

"Okay, okay." Kaley crossed to the pantry and grabbed a large can of tuna. After she retrieved the can opener from its drawer, she cut open the lid and split the tuna between the cats' bowls.

She wasn't sure if it was the sound of the can opener or the scent of the tuna that attracted Teller, but he strolled into the kitchen a second before she set their bowls on the food mat in the corner by the refrigerator.

"It's good to see the training is going well," Jo commented.

"You can't train cats," Kaley shot back.

"I meant Penn's training of you," Jo said.

The golden tabby looked up from his half-eaten tuna and meowed in obvious agreement.

Kaley sat down at the table again and continued paging through Grandma Charlie's Book of Shadows. Damn, she hated being stuck at home instead of going to Kirsten's basketball game. Maybe she shouldn't have let River heal her last night. But if he hadn't, she wouldn't have been in any shape to go to the game.

But on the other hand, she didn't miss the pain. An odd thought occurred to her. Did River's mom know about his healing abilities? If she did, is that the real reason she forced him to move back to

Millersburg? Had he tried to heal the damage to his grandmother's heart?

She pulled out her phone and stared at the screen. No new texts. Kirsten would still be on the court, but Kaley had hoped Donny or River would . . .

Dammit! She was not attracted to River Martin. He was in the same crappy situation a lot of other teens were in. Single parent raising him. Moving to a new school in the middle of the year because of his mom's job. And her mom's reaction toward him topped the cake. Was she feeling this way because of Mom and Jo's intense bigotry toward the fae in general?

Kaley sighed. Maybe she should text Josh and see if he was still coming over tomorrow after school to keep her company.

"Forbidden fruit is always the most luscious," Jo murmured.

"What?"

Jo looked directly at her. "I don't need to read your mind to know you're thinking about the Martin boy."

"Actually, I was thinking about him and Donny both." She grimaced. "Do witch guys go around knocking up Normal women without telling the Normal what they are?"

"What?" Jo's eyes widened.

Kaley shrugged. "Donny's mom had no idea his dad was a were. It wasn't her fault he went and got himself killed. But the same thing happened with River's mom. Kirsten and I are lucky Mom was honest with Dad. I can't imagine Mom abandoning us, then Dad raising us alone to find out by accident we have these abilities."

Jo cocked her head. "What does that have to do with male witches?"

"If the were and the fae men pull that kind of crap to have sex with Normal women, then what's stopping the witch guys from doing it, too?" Kaley took a deep breath because the last thing she wanted to do was hurt her aunt. "Isn't that why both you and Mom got divorced? Your husbands were cheating on you?"

"Oh, honey." Jo shook her head. "Cheating and deliberately impregnating a Normal woman are two different things."

"Is it?" Kaley regarded her aunt. "How many kids did your ex have with his Normal secretary before your divorce and after?"

Jo pursed her lips. "Not every male witch is like Dexter. And in your mom's case, she and Preston got married way too young. They grew apart. Besides, male witches are generally smart enough not to screw around on someone who can hex them."

"But you've always said hexes are a bad thing, and we should never use our abilities to harm someone," Kaley said.

Jo scowled at her. "Are you being a smartass on purpose tonight?"

Kaley crossed her arms. "I'm not the one freaking out about a fae in town. Maybe I would take you a little more seriously if you'd acted the same way with Donny."

Jo sighed. "I did."

"What?"

"I chewed your dad a new one about letting Donny play with you girls when you were in kindergarten."

"So, what made you change your mind about him?"

For an instant, guilt flashed across Jo's face. "I haven't. I still think he pretends to be your friend to get into your pants."

Oh, Goddess! Kayley roared with laughter until tears streamed down her face. If adults were this ridiculous, maybe she shouldn't be in a hurry to turn eighteen.

"What is so damn funny?" Jo demanded.

"I can guarantee he's not interested in me." Kaley reached for a bear claw from the box of pastries her aunt had brought over. "And I've been hoping Josh Fairbanks would ask me out, but my injuries from the explosion last night may have nixed any possibility of that."

"Normal men like damsels in distress," Jo huffed.

Kaley rolled her eyes. "More like he's trying too hard to be a gentleman, especially around Mom. People in this town are scared of her." She held up her free palm when Jo opened her mouth. "They were scared of her before we were outed. And some of the folks doing stupid stuff, like Principal Reed, have good reason to be afraid of her." She picked off a couple of almond slivers and popped them in her mouth. "She threatened his job last month when he attempted to suspend me after Amelia Ryder tried to slap me."

"Threatened him with magick?" Jo asked.

"No! Give her a little credit." Kaley chewed and swallowed the almond slivers. "She threatened to go to the school board because he wasn't following the student guidebook."

"Then Lester Reed should be worried about his job." Jo sipped her tea. "The incident with you and Amelia isn't the only time he's played favorites among the students and parents."

"Who else has he screwed over?"

"I'm not gossiping, young lady," Jo chided. "I just keep my ears open at my café. All you need to know is he's slime, and you need to steer clear of him and keep your nose clean until graduation. That means you stop skipping classes."

"Yes, ma'am." Kaley prayed her aunt would drop the subject. She'd had enough lectures from Mom and Dad.

Someone banged furiously on the front door.

She exchanged a look with Jo. Okay, she never had the Goddess answer a prayer that fast before.

"Get your sling and get on the couch," Jo whispered.

The banging started again. A voice yelled, "Hello! Is anyone home?"

Kaley ran to the couch, pulled on the sling the hospital had sent home with her before she plopped onto the cushions and arranged the throw over her legs. She nodded at Jo.

Magick whispered across Kaley's skin as her aunt pulled the door open.

"Can I help you?" Jo demanded.

"Hi, I'm Heather Martin," the woman's voice said. "I'm looking for my son River. He said he was having dinner here tonight."

"They're still at the girls' basketball game," Jo said. "Is there something wrong?"

"Oh, god." Ms. Martin groaned. "I was hoping he was here already. There was an explosion at the high school."

Chapter 20

Kirsten and Mom entered the much warmer school to find both the West Holmes and Indian Valley teams standing in the hallway and talking excitedly. All the basketball players shut up abruptly at the sight of the Wilsons.

To Kirsten's surprise, Tacy was the first to approach her. Indian Valley's lead scorer held out her fist. "Awesome game, Wilson, but I don't think I can beat you in the heroics department."

Kirsten fist-bumped her. "How about we skip the explosive devices and stick to the same bet when we come to your school in January?"

Tacy laughed while both team's coaches glared at the girls.

"There will be no gambling of any kind," Coach Park barked. Her counterpart of the rival high school Coach Nelson added, "That's for damn sure. Summers, you're sitting with me on the bus."

"Coach, you got it all wrong," Tacy said. "Wilson and I only bet with pop."

"And it's only about which of us scores more points," Kirsten added.

"I don't care," Coach Park said. "Do you two have any idea how much trouble you can get into by gambling? Do you know how many years Art Schlichter spent in prison? He started gambling in high school, too."

"Who's Art Schlichter?" Olivia asked.

The two coaches exchanged looks before Coach Park turned back to Olivia. "No one any of you should emulate if you want to continue to play basketball in our league. Look him up on the internet."

Kirsten wanted to melt into the floor. Mom didn't interfere, which meant she agreed to with Coach Park. It also meant Kirsten could expect another scolding from Mom on the way home. Getting chewed out after saving everyone's lives at the game wasn't the response she wanted. But on the other hand, the coach's lecture had nothing to do with her witchy abilities.

"We're sorry, Coach." She glanced at Tacy, who looked as remorseful as she felt. "We won't do it again."

"Lynn, what happened after Donny pulled the hex off the Fairbanks boy?" Mom asked.

Coach Park shook her head. "I don't know. Ethan and Doctor Timmons were working on him when law enforcement cleared the rest of us out of the gym."

"Is it all right if Kirsten cleans up and changes her clothes?" Mom jabbed her thumb in the direction of the door and the crater in the school yard. "We are supposed to go back out and give a statement to the cops."

Coach Park nodded. "I guess so. Law enforcement sent us back here."

Coach Nelson clapped her hands once. "All right, ladies. Hit the showers. You've got ten minutes. Hopefully, we can get you home before midnight."

Kirsten followed the rest of the Lady Knights into the women's locker room. Once the door swung shut, she tugged on Hope's sleeve. "Um, not to be stupid, but who won the game?"

The blonde laughed. "Too busy trying to save the world?"

Kirsten grinned at her friend's teasing. "No, just my sister's crush."

Olivia snapped Kirsten with her towel. "I can't believe you totally missed my perfect game-winning shot."

The rest of the team whooped and cheered as they stripped off their sweat-soaked uniforms. And Kirsten was rather glad Olivia was alive to get all the accolades she deserved.

When Kirsten exited the locker room, Mom was still waiting in the hallway. "You okay?"

"Yeah." Kirsten shook her head. "I got some well-deserved teasing for not knowing who won the game." She inclined her head toward the exit doors. "Shall we get the interrogation over with?"

"Actually, Chief Hall and Sheriff Birkheimer are meeting us at the house," Mom said as they walked down the hall toward the main doors. "Pat even offered to pay for and pick up the pizzas at McKelvey's."

"But this is an official investigation," Kirsten said as they backtracked toward the main entrance.

"And the majority of parents attending the game understand your quick thinking saved their children's lives."

Kirsten glanced at Mom. She definitely wore a scowl.

Time to change the subject before Mom started ranting about the principal again or remembered to lecture her about her bet with Tacy. "Did you text Dad to see how Josh was doing?"

"He's alive." Mom swallowed hard. The incident scared her more than she was willing to admit. "The paramedics let Donny ride with Josh to the hospital. His presence was the only thing keeping Josh calm. Your dad called Josh's parents, and he ran home for clean clothes and to pick up a change for Donny before he meets them at the hospital."

It wouldn't be the first time Dad had come home covered in blood, but it had always been animal blood when he was trying to save livestock or someone's beloved pet. This was . . .

Different.

The two incidents didn't match. The Painter Building was one thing. No one was inside besides the culprit. Kaley's injuries wouldn't have been as bad if she had just stayed in the frickin' car.

However, someone deliberately mixed magicks and planted the

hex on Josh to hurt or kill him. Maybe the culprit didn't realize Josh would be at the game. Or maybe they hoped to injure or kill anyone around Josh.

Like her own sister. It wasn't a secret around school that Kaley liked Josh. What if whoever was behind the mixed-magick explosions was really after Kaley?

Amelia's dad had an eclectic witch on his payroll. He threatened to sic his hired witch on Kaley after Amelia busted her knee trying to take a swing at Kaley last month. But Kirsten didn't think the freelancer working for the Ryders would be stupid enough to cross Brown Dog Coven.

But where did the fae portion of the hexes come from? That left River as the only fae they knew of in Holmes County. But for some reason, she was beginning to trust him. Besides, why would he draw attention to himself by setting off the mixed magick hexes? Especially with the relatively recent Unseelie crap in the county. Master Dare may hate Master St. James's guts, but she wouldn't allow the Winter Queen to mess with a witch coven in her territory.

Which left Josh himself as the target.

Who had it out for him? He was one of the few guys who got along with everyone at school. In fact, Josh's dad hired Donny during hay season based on Josh's recommendation.

Mr. Fairbanks actually worked as an accountant for Safewide, but he was determined to keep the family farm running, too. He often joked that farming was an expensive hobby, but that hobby gave his kids and Donny a more realistic look at life than slaving away in an office like he did.

That thought brought her full circle to Donny riding with Josh in the ambulance. He might not have any dinner if he didn't come to the Wilson home tonight.

"Donny's tight with Josh," Kirsten said. "We need to save him some pizza. He might not leave the hospital tonight."

"We will." Mom chuckled. "And here I thought Josh was sitting with us because he likes your sister."

"Oh, he definitely was. Donny was just a good excuse."

Mom cleared her throat before she added, "River Martin followed the ambulance to the hospital. I'm sorry I gave Kaley a hard time, and I'm sorry I planned on giving you a lecture tonight after the game."

"I had my own doubts about him," Kirsten admitted. "But he seems to be determined to prove he had nothing to do with the Painter Building."

She pushed open one of the main doors and a blast of cold air smacked her in the face. Out in the parking lot, the firefighters were rolling up their hoses while the officers from the police and sheriff's departments took statements from the remaining spectators.

Mom waited until they were safely ensconced in her dented sedan before she said, "Maybe we should be worried about him. What if he planted that hex because he wanted Josh out of the way?"

"I don't think so." Kirsten buckled her seatbelt. "High school soap opera crap is one thing, but it doesn't explain the Painter Building."

"Maybe River was testing the hex."

Kirsten glanced at Mom. "Or what if someone knows exactly what River is? Someone who wants some payback, and he oh-so-conveniently moved to a place where the Unseelie can't come. The real culprit has someone to take the blame for the harm they inflict. I think tonight's real target was Josh or both him and Kaley."

"Are you sure?" Mom asked as Kirsten started the car.

Was she? The bombing happened on River's first day at school. Why the hell would he start off doing things to attract attention to himself? Especially since most of the supernaturals in the U.S. knew about the Unseelie's attempt to destroy the vampire's goddess of death during the Battle of Millersburg. It was something to ask River about if he did come to the Wilson home for dinner tonight.

She glanced at Mom again before she pulled out of her parking space in the student section of the parking lot. "The fae don't claim their children by Normals, right?"

"As far as I know," Mom said tentatively.

Two deputies were still directing traffic at the entrance to the West Holmes High School and Junior High grounds. Though the deputy on Kaley's right waved her forward, she automatically checked both ways before she turned south onto the state route.

"It just seems to be a little too convenient all the trouble started right after the Martins moved back to town," Kirsten said. "Especially when whoever is behind the attempt to kill everyone at the game used one of Tina's charms for its witch magick."

"What?" Mom's shock jabbed at Kirsten's mind.

"You didn't see it?"

"I didn't get a good look at the physical item." Mom was silent for a long moment. "That explains why the witch magick felt familiar."

"We need to take a closer look at the Painter Building now that I know what I'm looking for," Kirsten said.

"Not without Pat and Jimmy's knowledge," Mom said.

"Of course not," Kirsten shot back. "I understand the chain of command with both departments."

"What's that supposed to mean?" Mom snapped.

Kirsten took a deep breath to settle her own irritation. "I get Principal Reed is a butthead. Every student at West Holmes knows he's a butthead. But you can't keep threatening him, Mom."

"After his blatant violation of the school rules when Amelia Ryder tried to strike my daughter—"

"And you won't let that go," Kirsten pointed out. "Not even when Kaley screwed up by skipping a class."

"Do I need to ground you, too?" Mom growled. "I was going to let the gambling thing go, but if you are going to pull attitude with me—"

"Is that the path you really want to take?" Kirsten asked mildly. "You're the one who keeps telling us that we need to be good examples of supernaturals among Normals."

Mom seethed for a few seconds before she sighed. "I hate it when you and your sister throw my own words back in my face."

"It's not our fault you give good advice." Kirsten slowed for a red light. "I think someone's setting up River and using Tina's charms to do it."

"But why?"

The light turned green, and Kirsten pressed the accelerator. "That's the million-dollar question, isn't it?"

Chapter 21

Shaking off the initial shock of the news of another explosion in town, Kaley said, "Don't make Ms. Martin stand out in the cold, Jo."

"I'm sorry. I forgot my manners." Her aunt gestured for their guest to enter the house.

River's mom was a tall woman dressed in jeans and a black wool coat that ended at mid-thigh. She exuded an air of conventional glamor when she stepped into the living room. Her dark brown hair was cut in a chin-length bob. Both cats hissed at River's mom before they raced upstairs.

Mom always said to pay attention to their familiars. Kaley wondered if Teller and Penn could smell River's fae essence on his mom. But neither cat had been upset with River himself last night. Maybe Ms. Martin was a dog person.

"I'm sorry for delivering bad news like this," she said. "I was on the way back to our hotel room when the DJ made the announcement. When River didn't answer his cell phone, I was really hoping he was having too much fun here to answer me."

"Let me text my parents and sister." Kaley tried not to imagine a repeat of what happened at the Painter Building last night. She was damn lucky to be alive, and she knew it. If something happened to her family . . .

"I'll do it, sweetie," Jo said as Kaley flung back the blanket.

Whoops. "Yeah," she muttered. "My shoulder just reminded me that wasn't one of my better ideas."

Jo pulled her phone out of her jeans pocket. Her one-finger typing was agonizingly slow as she entered the message. She looked up at River's mom. "I was about to make some more tea for myself. Would you like a cup while we wait for an answer, Ms. Martin?"

"Please, call me Heather." Her smile was rather weak, and anxiety bled off her. "Actually, some tea sounds very good right now."

"Have a seat, Ms. Mart—" At her raised eyebrow, Kaley amended her offer. "Heather."

River's mom nodded. "Thank you. You're Kaley, right?"

She nodded. "It's nice to meet you."

Heather perched on the armchair to Kaley's right. "River said you were the only one who was nice to him on his first day at West Holmes."

Kaley squelched the urge to shrug. "Folks in our county can be rather insular, but you probably know that since you grew up here. The other kids will get used to him."

Heather shook her head. "I do understand the insular part. It's one of the reasons I left."

"My sister talks about leaving, too," Kaley said. A soft buzz tickled the back of her mind amidst the banging in the kitchen. Jo was trying to contact Mom via telepathy. The answering buzz carried Mom's essence, but whatever the senior members of the family were discussing, they were deliberately leaving out Kirsten, not just Kaley.

"What about you?" Heather asked. "Have you decided what you are doing after graduation?"

Kaley delivered her normal reply to that particular question. "I still have a year and a half before I'm done with high school."

"It goes by faster than you think." The typical answer from adults.

"Our parents are pushing college," Kaley admitted. "I'm considering a couple of different majors, but at the moment, fashion marketing is at the top of my list."

The sound of the back door opening was followed by Jo's screech. "Goddess, Ethan! Please tell me that blood isn't yours!"

"Calm down, Jo," Dad barked. "It isn't mine. I need to change and take some clean clothes to the hospital for Donny."

Kaley threw off the blanket, jumped up, and ran to the kitchen.

Sure enough, Dad stood in the mud room. Blood soaked the front of his shirt. Additional splotches decorated his jeans. He was already stripping off his clothes.

"What happened? How bad was Donny hurt? We heard about the explosion at the high school."

Dad held up his palms. "Slow down, honey. I'm fine. Everyone's fine except for Josh Fairbanks. He's on his way to the hospital. Donny rode in the ambulance with him."

"Is River all right?" Ms. Martin said from behind Kaley.

Air froze in her lungs as she waited for Dad's answer, but his expression turned into mortification. He grabbed his bloody jeans out of the laundry sink and held them over his boxers.

"And you are?" he asked.

Kaley winced. "This is River's mom, Heather Martin. She came here because the police rerouted traffic, and he told her he was coming here after the game."

"Can I get dressed, Ms. Martin? Then I'll be happy to talk to you," he said.

"O-of course." The equally mortified woman practically ran into the dining room.

Dad yanked the mudroom door shut while Jo snickered as she poured hot water from the kettle into the two mugs on the counter.

"It's not funny," Kaley muttered.

"Neither is you running through the house like you weren't in any pain," Jo replied. "You know your parents are going to send you to school now." She carried the two mugs of tea into the dining room.

Kaley groaned and pulled off the stupid sling. Jo was right. She'd really screwed up in front of River's mom. But did she admit that River healed her? How much did Ms. Martin know about her son's abilities?

Dad opened the mudroom door. His cheeks were still pink, but he wore one of his OSU sweatshirts and clean jeans. "Next time, a little warning we have company would be nice."

"I'm really sorry." Kaley tried to look contrite. "I was afraid you'd been hurt. No one's been answering my texts."

Dad crossed to her and laid a hand on her shoulder. "I'm sorry we scared you, sweetheart." He glanced in the direction of the dining room before he looked at her again and lowered his voice. "How about we calm down River's mother before we talk?"

Kaley nodded. How had things gotten so screwed up this week? And why wasn't she as scared for Josh as she had been for River?

She followed Dad into the dining room. Jo had obviously been trying to comfort Ms. Martin. A tissue box and several crumpled tissues sat on the table between the two women.

"I'm Ethan Wilson, and I sincerely apologize, Ms. Martin." Dad smiled and held out his hand. "I don't usually greet guests in an undressed state."

Ms. Martin shook his hand. "Please, call me Heather. It's all right. I'm the one who barged in on your family in my panic after hearing the report on the radio."

"I can assure you River is fine." Dad waved in the general direction of the hospital. "He followed the ambulance to Pomerene to make sure Donny had a ride home." He made a face at Kaley. "My daughter likes to be the school's welcome wagon. She made her friends Donny and Josh be nice to River, which is why he was sitting with us during the game. And I apologize for the state of your son's clothing. Soak them in cold water before running them through the washer with some stain remover."

"Wh-what about the explosion that was reported?" Ms. Martin said.

"There was an explosion, but it happened outside of the school." Dad shook his head. "Luckily, Josh was the only one who was hurt. I can't really tell you anything more at this time. I assure you the

Millersburg Police Department and the Holmes County Sheriff's Department are working together to investigate the incident."

"The authorities say they are there to help, but they often drop the ball," Ms. Martin said bitterly.

"Sheriff James Birkheimer has been my best friend since our own high school days." Dad inclined his head toward Kaley. "And my daughter, his goddaughter, was injured in the bombing of the Painter Building last night. Trust me when I say he'll do everything in his power to catch the culprit."

Ms. Martin nodded at the same time her phone beeped. She pulled it out of her purse and thumbed the controls. "It's River, saying he's all right. He's asking if it's still okay that he has dinner here." She looked up at Dad. "I don't want to impose any more than we already have on your family—"

"It's okay if he comes for dinner." Jo laughed. "We've fed all of Kaley and Kirsten's friends at one time or another."

"Why don't you go back to your hotel room, and take a nice long soak in the tub?" Kaley said. "I've some unopened bath products and candles I can give you." She jumped up and ran up the stairs.

The cats watched her from between the bannisters, which was weird. Normally, they'd be curled up and asleep on hers or Kirsten's bed. Or hiding under one of the beds, considering their hissing act earlier. Penn emitted a questioning meow.

"Everyone's okay except Josh," Kaley said. The relief that River was uninjured swept through her again. It was an emotion she didn't want to examine too closely. She'd only met the guy yesterday for crying out loud.

The cats followed her into the bathroom and rubbed against her legs while she collected the bath bomb, shower gel, and matching lotion in a handled bag. She gave them each a quick ear scratch before she ran down the stairs.

Dad and Ms. Martin waited by the door.

"Here you go." Kaley handed Ms. Martin the bag. "Enjoy your evening."

"Thank you." She smiled at Dad. "And thanks for letting me know my son was all right."

"You're welcome," Dad said. "Rachel and I share the same worry over our own children."

Kaley and Dad watched Ms. Martin walk to her car and climb inside. A few seconds later, her sedan headed down the street.

"Let me get my coat and shoes, and I'll come to the hospital with you," Kaley said as Dad shut the front door.

"No," he said sternly. "I know you're feeling fine after River healed you, but I don't feel like explaining your miraculous recovery to the doctors and nurses tonight."

"But—"

"I said no, Kaley." He didn't raise his voice often, but the worry and fear emanating from him said his yelling wasn't from anger.

"I'm sorry." She swallowed the lump in her throat before she added, "I'm worried, too."

"I know, sweetie." He kissed her forehead. "Pat and Jimmy are on their way here, and your mom and Kristin should be home soon with the pizzas. Let me collect the boys, and check on Josh. I'm sorry he got hurt. If he can have visitors, I'll take you to see him tomorrow." Dad strode back to the kitchen.

Crap, that meant she was still grounded. How the heck did things get so screwed up this week?

Chapter 22

Kirsten pulled into their driveway. Dad's truck wasn't there. "Think he's still at the hospital?"

"That would be my guess," Mom murmured.

"Wanna tell me why you and Jo deliberately shut me out?"

Mom sighed. "She and Kaley found out about the explosion at the high school from River's mom. Apparently, she showed up on our doorstep, hoping he was here."

"That's why Kaley's been texting me constantly." Kirsten pushed the button to kill the engine. "That's not why you were shutting me out."

"Sweetie, you may not be technically working for the joint task-force yet." Mom hesitated for a moment before she blurted, "But I have my own suspicions about the magick bombs, but I don't want to influence you or the police or sheriff's departments through you."

"You've already affected me." Kirsten stared at the garage. "Kaley's right. I picked up yours and Jo's bigotry."

"That's not—"

Kirsten held up a hand to stop Mom's protest. "I'm not blaming you. You have every right to your feelings about the fae after what they did to the Normals in the county. But it doesn't make Kaley wrong. River didn't have a damn thing to do with the explosion at the Painter Building, and Donny proved it this afternoon." A bitter chuckle forced its way out of her throat. "As much he and I both wanted to discover otherwise."

"Are you sure?" Mom said.

"What if someone's taking a page from the Winter Queen's play-book?" Kirsten asked in return. "What if River is being set up?"

"Why would someone set up a high school kid?"

Kirsten shrugged. It would be best not continue pushing River's heritage and Mom and Jo's own attitudes. "That's a good question. If we can discover the motive, maybe we can figure out who's behind everything." She shivered. "Let's go inside. It's too cold to discuss this in your car."

Mom laughed. "I was about to say the same thing."

As they climbed out of her car, a sheriff's SUV pulled to the curb in front of the Wilson home, followed by a pickup. Chief Hall climbed out of the burgundy truck. Uncle Jimmy jumped out of his work vehicle and jogged to the passenger side of the chief's pickup.

"Need some help, Jimmy?" Mom asked.

"Actually, yes." He pulled out four pizza boxes from the stack in the chief's passenger seat. "I had Pat get a couple of extra pizzas for the boys. Didn't know if River eats like Donny does. But with tonight's excitement, I figured better safe than sorry."

"That's sweet of you," Mom said, nodding to both Jimmy and Chief Hall. "And thank you to both of you for picking up our dinner."

"For me, it's a working dinner." Chief Hall's wry smile reminded Kirsten the real reason the chief and Jimmy were here.

Hope rolled past them in her ancient Jeep and parked in front of Jimmy's SUV. She jumped out and ran up the sidewalk. "Woo-hoo! I'm just in time for the food."

Kirsten and Hope grabbed the rest of the boxes. Kirsten's stomach growled as they headed up the sidewalk, a reminder she'd worked off more power than just the basketball game.

Nervous energy bled off Kaley when they entered the house. "Dad just texted he and the guys are heading back now that Josh's family are at the hospital. What the heck happened? He didn't say much because River's mom was here."

"River's mom was here?" Mom paused, and her eyebrows rose.

"She heard about the explosion on the radio." Kaley wrung her hands. "River told her he'd be here tonight for supper."

"Maybe we should give him a pizza and send him home." Mom continued into the kitchen.

"He's assisting us with the investigation at the Painter Building," Kirsten bit out. "He has every right to be included in this meeting."

"Not to mention, Donny ruled out the possibility of the Martin kid being anywhere near the Painter Building prior to the explosion according to Julia," Jimmy said.

"What makes you so sure?" Mom snapped.

"Thad and Steve are enforcers," Jimmy set his boxes on the kitchen table. "Julia's been trained by Mai Osaka, same as her dad and stepbrother, and Mai's one of the best Normal enforcers, if not the best. So, give Julia a little credit."

"And situations like this are why I wanted to put together this joint taskforce," Chief Hall said.

"You weren't there when the Unseelie—" Mom started.

"And neither were you! You were huge and pregnant with the twins!" It wasn't often Uncle Jimmy lost his temper. "I was, and I'm not holding a racist grudge against a kid who wasn't even born yet!"

Chief Hall and Aunt Jo exchanged nervous looks. Even Kaley and Hope appeared equally uncomfortable.

"If the adults are finished throwing hangry temper tantrums, how about we eat?" Kirsten set the boxes she carried on the table next to Jimmy's stack. "Kaley, you wanna grab plates and napkins. Hope, you know where the soft drinks are. I'll get glasses. Who wants ice?"

What the heck happened tonight? Kaley asked silently.

Someone planted a mixed magic bombs on your crush, Josh, Kirsten replied. *And they used one of Tina's charms to do it.*

Chapter 23

Kaley rubbed her forehead. No wonder Mom was in a nasty mood. She viewed Tina Eisler as her little sister. Tina had ended up in the foster system after her mother died of a heroin overdose. She didn't have a clue who her father was. Mom had recognized Tina as a fellow witch when the girl had applied for a job at the *Monitor* after she graduated from high school.

At least, Tina had stopped screwing around and paid more attention to her children after Kaley and her twin discovered both kids were dreamwalkers. Tina's maternal instinct limited Kaley's babysitting income, but Mila and Noah needed Tina more than Kaley needed the cash.

That's going to screw with Tina's income if she can't sell her jewelry, Kaley said.

Jo sells trinkets at Nana's Gift Shop, too, Kirsten pointed out. *It could have just as easily been one of hers.*

"Want to share what you two are discussing?" Jimmy glared at them. His arms were folded across his chest, a hint he wasn't going to take any excuses.

"Kirsten was describing the fae charm that had been added to the necklace in Josh's pocket," Kaley answered. "Whoever is setting these hex bombs are using the good luck pieces Aunt Jo and Tina Eisler sell at Nana's Gift Shop as their source of witch magick."

"What?" Jo bellowed. Her face turned bright red. "How dare—"

"The girls mean we need to call Nana first thing in the morning and have her pull all of yours and Tina's merchandise," Mom interjected. "We also need to call Tina and warn her of what's going on."

"And now that I've seen one intact and in action, I need to go back to the Painter Building to perform another check," Kirsten added. "Can Deputy Wolford and the rest of the team meet me there before school tomorrow?"

Chief Hall nodded sharply. "Absolutely."

"Goddess," Jo swore. "What about all the pieces we've sold over the years?"

"My question is why did he have one of Tina's silver and purple quartz necklaces in his pocket." Kirsten eyed Kaley.

"What are you looking at me for?" she shot back.

"Really?" Kirsten cocked her head. "He stopped by here last night after you were released from the hospital. He sat with Mom and Dad at the game tonight. I'm worried someone is using him to get back at you for some reason."

A shiver ran through Kaley. "How could the explosion last night be aimed at me? No one knew we were stopping at the auto parts store except for the guys that work there and our parents."

"Why do you think your sister is the target?" Chief Hall asked quietly.

"Right now, just circumstantial evidence, ma'am." Kirsten's chin jutted up. "But Art Ryder threatened to sic his eclectic on Kaley last month after his daughter Amelia tried to slap Kaley, missed, and screwed up her own knee."

Chief Hall turned to Jimmy. "Did you know about this?"

Jimmy nodded. "It happened at Pomerene Hospital. He was stupid enough to do it in front of me."

Kaley turned to Jo and Mom. "Would an eclectic be crazy enough to mix magicks?"

The older women exchanged looks.

"I don't know of any witch who'd do that," Mom said.

"Wait a minute. What if I'm not the target?" Kaley said. "What if someone's trying to set up River?"

"That was the other theory I'm working on," Kirsten admitted. "Fae like to play the long game. To bomb the Painter Building on River's first day at high school makes no sense."

"But he was raised by his Normal mother," Jo protested. "Maybe he doesn't think like an Unseelie."

"What happened to innocent until proven guilty?" Kaley snapped. "Even the International Council follows that rule!"

"Ladies, calm down." Jimmy said.

The back door opened, and Donny entered the house, wearing the clothes Dad took to the hospital.

"Dude, even I'm not stupid enough to tell a bunch of women to calm down," he stated.

Kaley rushed over to him and wrapped her arms around him. "I'm so glad you're okay."

"The runt gets a hug, but I don't?" River stood behind Donny. Blood splattered his shirt and jacket. A reminder of how bad things had been at the high school.

Kaley's wash of emotion made her tear up. "Everybody gets a hug tonight. And I'll give one to Josh, too, as soon as he's well enough."

"Wait a minute." Dad closed the back door. "Let's get River's clothes soaking with mine and Donny's." Like earlier, he closed the door between the kitchen and the mudroom.

Kaley turned and walked over to the pantry and grabbed the paper plates before she refilled the napkin basket. Kirsten and Hope took their cues to get out the soft drinks and glasses. Jimmy headed into the dining room and carried extra chairs into the kitchen. Donny followed his lead.

Kaley found herself sitting between Mom and Jo. They were rather obvious about it, but she wasn't about to raise a fuss where River could hear it. Sometimes, she wished she had her sister's forthrightness, but she was so damn tired of fighting with Mom and Jo today.

By the time, Dad and River exited the mudroom, everyone else was munching on pizza. Donny was halfway through one box all by himself.

Wearing one of Dad's t-shirts, River plunked down in the chair between Hope and Jimmy and reached for one of the boxes. "Wow! Pineapple and ham. And here, I feared the lack of culture in my mom's hometown."

Everyone stared at him.

"Geez, people." He shook his head as he pulled a couple of slices onto his plate. "I was just joking. Indiana isn't exactly the bastion of high society either."

"True," Jimmy said. "They have arsonists in Indianapolis just like here in Millersburg."

River froze before he could take a bite of his pizza.

"What are you talking about?" Kaley demanded.

"You want to tell them, kid." Jimmy eyed River.

He stared right back at the sheriff. "Juvenile records are supposed to be sealed, and I'm only sixteen."

Kaley's heart sank. She had trusted River. Stood up for him when her family accused him of causing trouble. "Wh-what is Uncle Jimmy talking about?"

Pink flared across River's skin, making his white hair stand out even more. He looked at Kaley. "Remember the teacher I told you about?"

She nodded.

"Someone started a rumor Mr. Crawford had seduced me." His anger was cold and deep. "It wasn't true, but nobody cared about the truth in Indianapolis either. He was suspended. And a few nights later, his house caught fire. His wife and two kids managed to get out, but he didn't because he tried to save their dog."

River turned back to Jimmy. "The fire investigator said it was arson, and I was the police's chief suspect."

Chapter 24

Guilt drowned Kirsten. This was her fault. Of course, Julia added River's information in her report to Jimmy.

"River, don't get mad at Jimmy. I was the one—" Kirsten started.

Her godfather held up his hand. "This isn't your responsibility, young lady. I would have ordered the background check without your suggestion to Julia. Heck, after the Battle of Millersburg, I would have done the same thing to Donny if Audrey Fryer had moved away, then came back to town."

He turned to River. "I would like to hear your side of the story. What exactly was your relationship with this teacher back in Indiana?"

Kirsten shifted to Second Sight and watched River's aura as he told his tale. Not once did the turquoise light surrounding him waver. She could feel Kaley, Mom, and Jo do the same. And when Donny laid down the slice of pizza he was munching on, she would have bet every dollar she had he was testing River's scent as well.

"Mom was at some business dinner that night, so I didn't have an alibi since I was home alone," River finished with a shrug. "According to the defense attorney Mom hired to represent me, all the cops had was circumstantial evidence."

A wave of sadness from him permeated Kirsten. It felt similar to the occasional melancholy Donny felt around Dad. Mr. Crawford must have been the closest River ever had to a male role model.

"If the Indianapolis authorities suspected the house fire was arson, did they find any evidence?" Dad asked.

Jimmy nodded. "Someone cut a hole in one of the windows of their Florida room and fed gasoline through it. All it took was a long grill match."

"That doesn't make sense," Kirsten protested. "Even if River were behind the incident in Indianapolis and the explosions here, why would he change his M.O.?"

"Arsonists usually don't," Chief Hall said. "Who did you talk to in Indianapolis?"

"Detective Forrester," Jimmy said. "He asked me point-blank if River was a supernatural."

River frowned. "Why? I've never said anything to anyone except Mr. Crawford until we moved to Millersburg, and Kaley knew right away what I was."

"Detective Forrester discovered the teacher who started the rumor about you and Mr. Crawford is a member of Humanity Now," Jimmy said.

Chief Hall whistled. "Well, that puts a different spin on things."

More worry gnawed on Kirsten's nerves. Granted some of it was Kaley's feelings. Being a witch was bad enough when separating her emotions from her friends and family, but the twin bond made things worse. However, Kirsten was pretty sure someone had found out both River and Mr. Crawford had fae blood.

"Crap," Dad muttered. "These idiots are all over the place these days, aren't they?"

"Could Humanity Now have learned about magick interaction?" Jo asked.

"But how could they?" Kirsten tried to pull the disparate threads of the different situations into a pattern she could understand, but it didn't make sense. Maybe there was still something missing. "It's not like the full-blooded fae would hand out bespelled items to random humans."

"But what if a half-fae is selling jewelry laced with a good luck charm like Tina does?" Kaley asked.

Everyone grew silent at Kaley's question. Everyone except Donny who was digging into his second pizza.

Jo's phone rang, and everybody jumped. She checked the caller ID.

"I need to take this." Jo hopped up and strode into the living room.

"This is going to limit Tina's income," Mom murmured.

"Why can't she make her jewelry without any spell attached to them?" Hope asked.

"Half the attraction for her pieces is because she's a member of a legitimate witch coven," Kirsten said.

Jo strode back into the kitchen. "Just a minute, Anne." She held her phone against her chest. "Anne Fitzgerald's on the line with Thad Wolford and Stan Gryffudd, the St. James head of Las Vegas. He's half-fae himself. They'd like to talk to all of us after I told them there had been a second mixed-magick explosion tonight. Is that okay?"

"Definitely," Jimmy said. "Pat, Anne's a former enforcer with the Western U.S. Vampire Coven, but she was born and grew up here."

Chief Hall chuckled. "I've heard the stories about her already."

Jo tapped the speaker function and sat at her place, holding her phone up so everyone at the table could hear. Everyone went around the table and introduced themselves before Jimmy filled them in on the two incidents in town.

"Mr. Gryffudd, is it possible someone who's half-fae might be selling charmed items?" Kirsten wanted to ask before Mom and Jo started any of their stupid bigotry. Miz Anne wouldn't have Mr. Gryffudd on the phone unless she trusted him.

"Usually not." He chuckled. "When I was your age, it was a good way to get burned at the stake. However, it doesn't mean someone who didn't know they have fae blood isn't doing exactly that."

"The witch-spelled object from tonight's explosion was made by the only witch who's not sitting at this table," Kirsten said. "And I'm darn sure Tina wasn't involved because she'd never endanger her two kids."

"Tina Eisler?" Thad asked.

"Yes," Jo answered. "She's grown up quite a bit since the last time you picked her up for drunk and disorderly. She manages the billing department at Pomerene Hospital now."

"How old are her children?" Thad asked.

"Noah's twelve and Mila's eight," Mom said. "But they can't possibly be behind the mixed magick bombs. They're both powerful dreamwalkers. We had to bind their powers."

"That doesn't mean they didn't get a hold of a couple of their mother's charmed accessories," Anne said.

"I can go over to the Eislers' place tomorrow night," Kaley said. "I've babysat them occasionally. Noah and Mila will talk to me."

"What about the Killbuck pack, Jimmy?" Thad asked. "There's nothing stopping them from meeting someone from the Winter Court outside of Holmes County. Both incidents involved Rachel's girls. If any of them still hold a grudge over Rachel helping us during the Battle of Millersburg, I wouldn't put it past them to hurt the twins and blame the Winter Queen."

Jimmy glanced at both Kaley and Kirsten before he said, "But why would the Killbuck pack wait seventeen years before going after the twins? Besides, Rachel wasn't involved directly in the battle. The pack has been more busy dealing drugs in an effort to raise money in order to attract new werecoyote ladies since the half the 'coyotes joined your missus to form the Las Vegas pack."

"I'll ask Leslie and the rest of the werecoyote staff here," Mr. Gryffudd said. "See if they've heard anything from their relatives."

Kirsten peeled a slice of crisp pepperoni from the top of her pizza and popped it into her mouth. It seemed like the adults were dredging up every possible enemy from their past instead of looking at the connections right in front of them.

Hope scribbled on her notebook and held it for Kirsten to read.

NONE OF THIS EXPLAINS WHY JOSH WAS TARGETED.

Kirsten looked at Hope and nodded. Good to know she wasn't the only one questioning the direction of the conversation. She laid her hand on Hope's arm.

Does speaking to you telepathically bother you?

Not a bit. Hope's laughter tickled the back of Kirsten's mind.

I think Josh may have bought that necklace for Kaley.

Hope took a swig of her root beer. *Have you asked Donny about it? Josh isn't exactly in a condition where we can ask him.*

Thanks for being logical.

Hope shifted to squeeze Kirsten's hand. *Hey, if it'd been one of my brothers injured in the Painter Building explosion, I wouldn't be thinking straight either.*

Donny?

What are you two gossiping about? He continued to munch on his slice of super meat pizza.

Did River tell the truth about what happened in Indianapolis? Kirsten crossed the fingers of her free hand.

Didn't you Look at his aura?

I want a confirmation, doofus.

Donny rolled his eyes. *Don't worry. Elf boy stayed honey sweet the whole time.*

"What are you kids talking about?" Jimmy demanded.

All the adults stared at Kirsten.

She took a deep breath. This may blow her internship to smithereens, but the bomber was going to kill someone if they weren't stopped. "I think you're on the wrong track. Our bomber has nothing directly to do with the Unseelie or River."

Chapter 25

Kaley stared at her sister. What the heck had prompted the change of heart after Kirsten threw a fit about River healing her last night?

"Has it occurred to any of you Humanity Now might be behind the death of River's teacher Mr. Crawford?" Kirsten gestured wildly. "Or that the real reason Heather Martin left Indianapolis was because she was worried about her son's safety? If Humanity Now has discovered the dangerous reaction of mixing magicks, they could be using it to sow distrust—"

"Whoa, girl." River held up his palms. "Mom got a promotion—"

"It's been nearly three months since Cissy had her heart attack," Jo said. "Why didn't the two of you come here when she was in the hospital?"

A confused expression crossed River's face, and Kaley's heart went out to him.

"I-I didn't know about my grandmother's condition until Mom told me a couple of weeks ago," he said. "I never met her before this past weekend. She and Mom didn't talk while I was growing up."

"I was in Cissy's hospital room when she called your mother in August," Jo said gently. "She didn't tell then?"

"I swear I didn't know my grandmother had been sick until a couple of weeks ago when Mom said we were moving to Millersburg." River's cheeks and ears turned pink, and anger flowed from him in deep, dark waves. "Look at my aura if you don't believe me."

"I am Looking," Kaley said. "And I believe you." She glared at Jo. "Why are you harassing him? And why aren't you listening to Kirsten? You guys are proving her point. You're picking on the only fae in town instead of looking at the evidence!"

"Don't you talk back to me—" Jo started.

"Jo, stop now," Dad barked. "The girls have a point."

Mom stared at Dad with an appalled expression. "Ethan—"

"Rachel, Ethan's right. The girls do have an excellent point," Jimmy added gently. "Crawford died shortly after Labor Day." He faced River. "When does school start in Indianapolis?"

River gulped. "First week in August."

Jimmy turned back to Mom. "Think about it. Put yourself in Heather's position, would you pull the girls out of school or leave them by themselves in a major city with no one around to call for help?"

"No," Mom muttered.

"Then cut both Heather and River some slack." Jimmy reached for another slice of pizza. "You know how Cissy is, and you know damn well she tossed Heather out of the house when the girl got pregnant. Frankly, I wouldn't jump at helping my own mother if she pulled that crap with me. Neither would you, Josephine, and we both know it." He watched Aunt Jo while he chewed.

Both her aura and her skin flared with her embarrassment, and she remained silent.

Kaley bit her lip. She could only imagine what Miz Anne, Julia's dad, and Mr. Gryffudd were thinking. The so-called adults in the kitchen seemed to forget the St. James members were on the phone.

Donny belched. "Since we're not going to talk about the Painter Building case, can you drop me off at the high school so I can pick up my car, River? I've got to finish reading Romeo and Juliet for English Lit."

"Donny, wait—" Chief Hall started.

"No problem." River stood. "Thank you for dinner, Mr. Wilson." He grabbed his coat and stiffly walked out of the kitchen.

Kaley leapt to her feet and ran after him. "River, wait!"

When she reached the living room, his hand rested on the front door's knob, but he wouldn't look at her.

"I'm sorry my mom and aunt were so rude to you." Emotions swirled around both Kaley and River. She wasn't sure what she could say to make things right.

"Kirsten and Hope are the smartest people we know." Donny entered the living room, slinging on one of Dad's extra jackets. Kirsten followed him with a grim expression. "If they see a connection behind your teacher's death and your mom getting you the hell out of Indiana, then you can bet your powers on it."

Kaley stepped closer to River. If her sister was right, he and his mom were in danger. "Do you know how to cast a ward?"

River shook his head. He still wouldn't look at her. "Let's go, Donny." He jerked the door open and stepped outside.

Kaley followed. "River, hold on a minute. I won't risk your life trying to teach you or ward your hotel room for you. I'll get Mr. Gryffudd's number. You need to learn from an experienced fae."

"Don't you mean half-fae?" River's anger wasn't aimed at her, but it still hurt.

"You can act like a jerk to me." Kirsten stepped between them. "I deserve it. But my sister doesn't. She's stood up for you from the moment she saw you."

Well, that wasn't totally true, but if Kaley corrected her twin, River would never speak to her again.

"Talking from experience here, dude," Donny said. "Kaley will help you whether you want her to or not. It's best to shut up and let her do it because you aren't going to stop her."

"And when both of you get home, text me so I know you're safe," she said.

Donny turned to Kirsten. "Text me if you do end up meeting Deputy Wolford at what remains of the Painter Building before school."

"I will." Kirsten nodded.

The guys strode down the porch steps and to River's Jeep. They climbed in, and the engine roared to life. Kaley stood beside her sister until the tail lights turned at the corner in the direction of Jackson Street.

"Is it just me, or are they being nice to each other?" Kirsten murmured.

"Yeah, they are." Kaley shook her head. "I think Donny chilled after he didn't pick up River's scent at the Painter Building this afternoon."

"I'm kinda feelin' the same way." Kirsten sighed, and her breath steamed in the night air. "It's too cold to debate this outside. Let's see if the adults are behaving. Otherwise, we'll grab Hope and hash things out upstairs in my room." She pivoted and stalked into the house.

Kaley stared up at the maple tree in front of their house. The same one River had climbed last night. If he hadn't done so, she'd be dead. Even Kirsten had enough healing sense to realize that.

From the emanations of her twin's emotional funk, Kirsten was irritated with Mom and Jo's behavior on top of everything else. Kaley couldn't blame her. Their family may have just screwed up Kirsten's internship, the one thing that would have kept her in Millersburg.

And for the first time, Kaley totally understood her sister's desire to get away from their family.

Chapter 26

When Kirsten returned to the kitchen, Chief Hall stood and held out a piece of paper. "Mr. Gryffudd left his number. Would you please give it to River? According to Mr. Gryffudd, he and River are at least cousins, if not half-brothers. He'd like to talk to River one-on-one."

"Thanks." Kirsten nodded. "I don't like my suspicions, but it would be nice for River to have a teacher so he can protect himself."

Kaley re-entered the kitchen and stood beside her. From the wash of relief, her sister heard the chief and was glad Mr. Gryffudd had voluntarily left his contact info.

Kirsten handed the slip to her twin. "You wanna text River?"

Kaley nodded.

"Also, I'll write the excuse for you, Hope, and the boys if we're still at the Painter Building after school starts," the police chief continued.

"You still want my help?" Kirsten held her breath, half-afraid to believe Chief Hall's words.

The officer stared at Mom and Jo as she spoke. "I think you, Kaley, and your friends proved my point tonight about recruiting younger supernaturals for conventional law enforcement investigations." She turned back Kirsten. "Your talents have been a big help. Not to mention, you and your friends impressed the heck out of Mark Hatfield today, and not much impresses him. Don't worry. You still have your internship offer, and it's already paying off for me." She smiled as she donned her coat. "You girls get some rest. And congratulations on tonight's basketball win."

"Thanks, Chief." Kirsten's aching lungs released the rest of their air as Hall left the kitchen.

Kirsten waited until she heard the front door open and closed before she turned to Mom. "What the heck was tonight really all about? You've known Miz Anne since before we were born. You and the Wolfords are friends. Why wouldn't you take their word Mr. Gryffudd is on the up-and-up?"

"That's what I'd like to know." Uncle Jimmy leaned back and crossed his arms.

"Jo and I have valid concerns—" Mom started.

"Bull . . . cookies," Dad snapped. "Cookies" was obviously not the word he wanted to use, but he watched his cussing around Aunt Jo.

"You don't understand, Ethan," Mom said, her voice rising with each word.

"This is not any different than the crap you and Jo pulled when the kids were five." Dad's clear and careful enunciation said how angry he was. "River is just as much of an outcast from the Winter Court as Donny is from the Killbuck Pack. Hanging to these generational grudges is not helping anyone. Especially a couple of kids with nowhere to go."

"You're young," Jo said. "You haven't seen the things we have."

"Let me take this one, Ethan." From the dark scarlet flares in Jimmy's cheerful red aura, he was as angry as Dad. "Here's the problem from the Normal perspective. Thad tells me about some of the crap he's seen since he started working for the St. James Coven. The supernaturals are out now. Your supernatural battles have spilled over and injured or killed civilians, and you can't cover it up anymore. What do you think is going to happen when us regular folks get tired of being on the receiving of your squabbles?"

"And who do you think the Normals will go after first?" Kirsten quietly added.

The adults all stared at her. Mom and Jo with varying degrees of horror. Jimmy with understanding. Dad with a sorrow that went beyond his expression at the ER last night when Kaley was treated for her injuries from the explosion.

"Sheriff Birkheimer and Kirsten are right, Miz Wilson," Hope murmured. "You may not hear some of the talk around town, but as a Normal, I do. Frankly, it scares me because I know Kirsten and Kaley would never hurt anyone intentionally, but that doesn't stop people from being afraid of you, Miz Jo, and them."

"Hope's right," Jimmy said. "Folks like Lewis Zarnecki don't like the idea of people who are weapons in and of themselves. And the deadliest predator in the world isn't a hungry vampire. It's a scared human."

"Well, I don't like Pat Hall's attitude," Jo shot back. "She wants to steal our children and train them like a Normal's hunting dog."

"Is that what you believe about me?" Kirsten blurted. "That I can't think for myself?"

"I didn't mean you girls," Jo protested.

"No, she meant everyone who's underage." Hope pushed to her feet. "My grandma talks the same way about supernaturals. I'll see you in the morning at the Painter Building, girl. For what it's worth, I think you're right about someone using River's presence to start some crap in town." She fistbumped Kirsten.

"'Preciate your help today."

Hope donned her coat and stalked out of the house without another word.

"I'm going to bed." Kirsten pivoted, but before she could take a step, Mom said, "Wait."

Kirsten turned back to face Mom. "Why? So you can insult local law enforcement, put me down, or make more of a fool of yourself in front of the St. James master of Las Vegas?"

"Don't you talk back to me—"

Exhaustion dragged on Kirsten. She didn't have the energy to fight anymore. "Mom, things are changing whether you and Jo like it or not. Gods run one of the U.S. vampire covens. There's a cure for the V-virus for those smart enough to take it. And if we don't start adhering to the spirit of the I.C. Accords, then Uncle Jimmy's right. The Normals will kill all of us supernaturals because we're too busy fighting among ourselves to pay attention. I'm sorry if you can't see that. But it's true."

She pivoted again and marched out of the kitchen before she did or said anything more. Along with the fatigue, she felt sad. Sad that she let Mom and Jo's bigotry infect her. All their stories painted most witches in righteous light. But now . . .

Now, she wondered if she would live long enough to have her own children.

Kirsten reached the top of the stairs to find the cats staring at her as if she were a total stranger. "Hey, guys."

The normally talkative Penn didn't meow. Teller padded after Kirsten to her room. Penn stared between the spindles for a moment before he followed his brother. Both felines were upset by something, but Kirsten couldn't pick out a specific reason from their emotions. It could simply be everyone yelling at each other around the kitchen table.

She changed into her pajamas before she trudged to the bathroom she shared with Kaley and went through her nightly ablutions. The quick shower she took at the high school meant she could sleep in an extra fifteen minutes. As she returned to her room, she could hear Mom, Dad, Jimmy, and Jo still arguing though she couldn't make out the words.

Kaley sat on Kirsten's bed, petting both cats. The boys sat rigidly straight on the purple comforter, not sprawled on their backs and demanding belly rubs like they normally did at bedtime.

"Mom and Dad kick you out of the kitchen smackdown?" Kirsten flopped on her bed beside her sister and the cats.

"No, I said my own piece about how Mom and Jo are treating River and Mr. Gryffudd." Kaley sighed. "Both River and Donny texted to say they are safe and sound at home. And River said thank you for giving him Mr. Gryffudd's phone number."

"How are you feeling?" Kirsten asked.

"Still tired from the healing." Kaley half-smiled. "But a fae healing is still better that the pain or the pills."

"I wonder if he's tried to help his grandmother," Kirsten mused.

Kaley snorted. "As much as Cissy Martin smokes and drinks, I doubt if there's anything even fae magick can do to fix her."

Kirsten stared at the ceiling. "I've got to apologize to him tomorrow. I didn't realize how much of Mom and Jo's bigotry I'd absorbed. It wasn't fair to him." She turned her head to see Kaley. "I wasn't fair to you either. I'm really, really sorry."

"It's okay." Kaley sighed again. "Finding out your parents aren't perfect is part of growing up."

"What I don't get was why River helped you, but he didn't help Josh."

Kaley laid on her side, her head propped on her left fist. "River texted he was feeling guilty about not trying to heal Josh tonight, but he was afraid he'd kill Josh with the mixed magicks making him sick."

"That was probably the smartest thing he could have done." An idea blossomed in Kirsten's brain. "Want to go visit Josh at the hospital after school tomorrow with me?"

"Dad said he'd take me tomorrow night."

"I think we need to talk to him sooner." Kirsten scowled at her twin. "You can blame me for breaking your grounding."

"And you'll claim Jimmy sent you to talk to Josh," Kaley teased before she frowned. "I do want to see him, but why do you want to go?"

"I want to find out who else might have touched that necklace he was carrying in his pocket."

Chapter 27

The next morning, Kaley couldn't argue when Mom and Dad insisted she go to school. However, she was on edge all during homeroom, but Hope never showed. Neither did anyone text Kaley about what they might have uncovered at the second search of the Painter Building this morning.

Fine. She could wait. However, every teacher between homeroom and lunch period lectured her about distracting the other students by bouncing her right heel.

After Kaley grabbed the most appetizing thing the lunch ladies were serving, she didn't see her twin sitting with the other basketball players in the cafeteria. She scanned the room, before she finally spotted Kirsten and Hope tucked in a corner at one of the smaller tables with River and Donny.

Kaley stalked over, set down her tray, and grabbed an empty chair from another table before she sat between Hope and River. "Since you were late to school, I'm assuming you guys found something."

Kirsten looked around them before she said, "Yeah, the fae magick definitely isn't River, and we found more of Tina's jewelry."

"At least what was left of it," Donny muttered. "Bits of silver and obsidian near where Chief Nicholls and the fire investigator think the explosion occurred."

"Damn," Kaley whispered. "They don't think she has anything to do with it, do they?"

"Jimmy already questioned her yesterday." Kirsten's worry flowed and melded with Kaley's own concerns. "He's cross-checking with Nana Strickland over which of Tina's consigned pieces had been sold before Chief Hall goes to the hospital to talk to Tina again this afternoon."

"And before you get your panties in a wad, neither Sheriff Birkheimer or Chief Hall thinks Tina or River are involved." Hope stated. "But they have to cross their t's and dot their i's because we have no clue of who's really behind this."

"What about your theory?" Kaley eyed her sister across the table while she bit into one of her chicken tenders.

Kirsten shrugged. "Jimmy's leaning toward the Winter Queen using River's presence to cause trouble. Chief Hall's the only one looking into Humanity Now."

Kaley swallowed her bite of chicken. "Zarnecki?"

The other four all nodded.

"We can't wait for the next bombing," Hope said. "You getting injured from the Painter Building's flying debris may have been an accident, but if the bomber knew Josh was going to last night's game, we're looking at attempted murder."

"Kaley and I are going to check on Josh after school." Kirsten shot a wry grin Kaley's way. "The coach cancelled this afternoon's practice. I'm assuming you're still banned from any afterschool activities."

Kaley nodded. In the current scope of crimes in town, her punishment for skipping a class seemed a ridiculous thing for the adults to get upset about. After Mom and Jo's behavior last night, she realized the actions of the adults were a desperate attempt to retain control of those they considered children.

"We should come, too," Donny muttered.

"Hospital visitation only allows two people at a time." Hope turned to Kirsten. "You two are going to do your own checking on Tina while you're there, aren't you?"

"Well, duh." Kirsten rolled her eyes.

But it was River's intense stare that caught Kaley's attention.

"If you detect any fae magick at the hospital, text me," he murmured.

"Why?" Donny asked with genuine curiosity.

"Mr. Gryffudd said I could call him any time, and he seems a little more level-headed than the adults here in Millersburg." River swirled his popcorn shrimp through his ketchup. "I trust his opinion after he walked me through warding my grandmother's house."

Hope frowned. "I don't understand. Why are you putting your faith in someone who lives on the other side of the country?"

"Because Mr. Gryffudd has no skin in this game, and neither he or River are trying to suck up to either court." Kaley dipped her half-eaten chicken tender in the cup of ranch dressing. "Why were you warding your grandma's house? I thought you guys were staying at the Holiday Inn until the moving truck from Indianapolis arrived."

"We moved in with Grandma last night." River grimaced as he chewed and swallowed his shrimp. "After I got back to our hotel room, I told Mom about Kirsten's theory concerning Mr. Crawford. She admitted she was worried whoever killed him might come after me next, which is the real reason why she took the promotion back here. After Mom told my grandmother what was really going on, Grandma insisted we move in with her."

Kaley sighed. "Well, Mr. Gryffudd seems willing to listen, and I'll take whatever real assistance we can get." Because, Goddess help them, none of her family seemed to care about getting to the truth.

"Anyone got plans for tonight since the boys have an away game?" Hope asked.

"I'm still grounded," Kaley grumbled.

"Why don't we make tacos at our place and watch a movie?" Kirsten suggested.

"That's not fair to River." Kaley glared at her sister. "Mom and Jo were mean enough to him last night."

"Why don't we go to my house?" Hope suggested. "Mom and Dad are taking Brian to the Cleveland airport tonight. If it's just us, they won't have a problem."

"And that's not fair to Kaley," River protested before he held up his hands. "Besides I promised my grandmother I'd move some furniture around tonight. We can get together at Hope's once Kaley's free." He grinned at her. "No more skipping classes. I need my tutor."

"It's a deal." She smiled back. Why, oh, why did she feel butterflies in her stomach at the looks he gave her? Josh didn't make her feel this way.

Normally, she could talk to Mom about this stuff, but poor River had a major strike against him that neither of them could change.

Kaley leaned against the trunk of Mom's car when Kirsten finally strode out to the parking lot.

"Took you long enough." Kaley straightened.

Kirsten pressed the fob in her hand, and the trunk latch popped. "Who peed in your cereal?"

Kaley pushed the lid up and dumped her backpack in the car. "You and Donny were total jerks to River, and now you guys are best friends."

"I'm not denying we changed our attitudes, but why aren't you happy now?" Kirsten tossed her backpack in the trunk and slammed the lid shut. "You're the one who told us to behave around him."

"I—" Reality smacked Kaley, and she swallowed hard as they both climbed into the front seats.

"I what?" Kirsten pressed the ignition.

"I don't like not being part of the formal investigation."

"You nearly died two days ago." Kirsten stared at her like she'd grown an extra head. "Yesterday, you were exhausted from the healing. It wasn't like I planned to exclude you."

"I know." Kaley twirled her thumbs. "I-I don't get you. A couple of weeks ago, you wanted to leave Millersburg to get away from me. Are you expecting me to leave now that you have a place in the police department?"

"What?" Kirsten's cheeks turned red. "That is the most ridiculous thing I've ever heard you say."

"So now I'm ridiculous?" Kaley shot back.

Kirsten paused with her hand on the gear shift. "Why are you trying to pick a fight now? You're coming with me to the hospital, aren't you? You've been laying enough hints to Josh. Heck, he came to see you when you got out of the ER the night—" She closed her eyes and leaned back against the headrest. "Oh, Goddess, I am so stupid."

"What?" Kaley couldn't figure out what was going through her sister's head, and Kirsten wasn't letting her in. Had Miss Superbrain finally blown a blood vessel?

"Look if you've changed your mind about how you feel about Josh, can you please wait until he's out of the hospital before you break his heart?"

"I haven't—" Kaley's protest died on her lips. She hadn't changed her mind. It was just—

Oh, heck! This was getting more complicated.

Kirsten opened her eyes and rolled her neck until she faced Kaley. "I have absolutely no interest in River either."

Kaley's face heated. "It's not the healing spell!"

"I know it isn't," Kirsten said softly. "But I wouldn't bring up your feelings in front of Mom or Jo." She straightened in the driver's seat. "Actually, don't say anything to Dad about your feelings for River either. You don't want to give him a reason to side with Mom."

"Except I can't talk to you about him either," Kaley grumbled.

"Like I said before, I'm absolutely not interested." Kirsten shifted the car into reverse and backed out of their assigned spot. "I'm starting to understand Chief Hall's reasoning though for recruiting younger supernaturals who aren't carrying a ton of their ancestral baggage."

As they joined the line of student vehicles leaving the parking lot, Kaley stared out the windshield. She really hoped that necklace in Josh's pocket hadn't been for her. It would make the guilt swirling through her that much worse.

Chapter 28

Kirsten pulled into a parking spot and cut the engine. Her twin's free-flowing guilt tasted like burnt toast, which explained Kaley's rare silence. Kirsten barely imagined liking one real-life guy, much less two at the same time, but then, she wasn't about to let romance get in the way of her life goals.

Not yet anyway.

"Just don't get Josh any flowers in the gift shop, and you'll be fine," she murmured as she yanked on the car door's latch.

"What if your original theory is right?" Kaley murmured.

Kirsten let the driver side door slam shut. "I seem to recall blaming River. Can you be more specific?"

"What if this is a plan by the Unseelie queen?" Kaley finally turned to face Kirsten. "Revenge against Mom and Jo for the Battle of Millersburg. The queen can't get to anyone from the St. James Coven. But there's a bunch of people that were a part of the battle against the sidhe who still live here. What if you were right I was the target? That means it's my fault Josh—"

"Stop." Kirsten held up her hands. "Stop right there."

"But—"

"We know nothing at this point. That's why we're here. We need to find out where Josh got that damn necklace and who might have touched it between Nana's shop and last night." Kirsten laid her hand on Kaley's arm. "It's this maniac's fault. Not yours. Unless you and River decided to become Bonnie and Clyde."

Kaley's eyes narrowed. "You can be a real jerk."

"That's what baby sisters are for." Kirsten smirked.

"Three minutes." Kaley held up the requisite number of fingers on her free hand. "I'm only older by three minutes." But the taste of her thoughts shifted more toward her normal cotton candy. "Thanks."

"For what?"

"Getting me out of my head."

Kirsten squeezed her sister's arm. "Let's go see Josh and Tina."

Kaley nodded.

Together, they climbed out of Mom's sedan and headed for the hospital's main entrance. At Kaley's insistence, they did stop at the gift shop. She bought a box of peanut butter cups. When Kirsten cocked an eyebrow, Kaley blushed.

"I don't want to go upstairs empty-handed," she snapped.

"You're assuming that necklace was for you," Kirsten murmured as they left the gift shop. "Do you really want to encourage Josh if you don't plan to go out with him?"

"You are taking this whole non-existent relationship way too seriously," Kaley grumbled. "We haven't even been on a date yet." She paused in the middle of the lobby. "Wait a minute. Don't we need to get his room number?"

"Donny already texted me the room number." Kirsten grinned at her sister. "You might want to try to keep up if you want to be part of this investigation."

"How'd Donny get the room number?" Kaley asked as they continued toward the elevators.

Kirsten couldn't resist teasing her twin. "There's this neat thing on your phone that sends actual words, and you can form questions on it."

"You are a jerk," Kaley muttered. "A big ole sarcastic jerk." She stabbed the button on the elevator panel. "You could have just said Josh is well enough to text Donny."

"And you could have deducted that's how I got Josh's room number."

"No, I would have to make the assumption the guys texted,"

Kaley shot back. "Donny could have just as easily called Josh's parents, or he could have visited prior to meeting up with you and your private detective squad this morning."

Kirsten chuckled. "I don't get why you think playing the dumb blond is a good idea. You're just as smart if not smarter than I am."

Kaley's shoulders slumped. "If I'm being honest, you're not the only one who feels like she's in her twin's shadow."

Well, crap. Kirsten stared at the tips of her tennies. No wonder Kaley had been pissy with her over the last couple of years. In her desperation to see the world, it hadn't occurred her sister would be feeling the same way. She sighed and looked at Kaley.

"I guess our problems stem from the same need to prove ourselves," Kirsten murmured. She didn't want to lay her emotions out in front of all the strangers gathered for the elevator. *Can we talk later?* she added silently.

That would be a good idea. Kaley nodded as the doors slid open.

Only after the car filled, the doors slid shut, and the elevator started its climb did Kirsten notice the other passengers kept as far from her and Kaley as they could in the crowded space.

For the first time, she found herself regretting she'd used her powers in front of people.

The door to Josh's room was closed when the twins reached it. Kirsten knocked softly before she opened it a crack and peeked around the edge. Mrs. Fairbanks looked up from her phone with a wan smile.

Josh snored in his bed. His skin was terribly pale except for the black, blue, and purple circles around his eyes. The transparent tube across his face hissed as it pushed oxygen into his nostrils.

Mrs. Fairbanks didn't look much better. Her skin had a gray-ish tinge, which brought out the lines on her face. She held her index finger to her lips and stood before she joined Kirsten and Kaley in the hallway and closed the door behind her.

"How's Josh doing?" Kaley asked.

"Better." Mrs. Fairbanks nodded. "It took a couple of transfusions. Apparently, your sister finding that necklace in his pocket and getting rid of it saved his life."

"Actually, it was Donny who found it," Kirsten said. "Um, that's one of the reasons we dropped by. Do you know where he got it?"

Mrs. Fairbanks shook her head. "I didn't know he had it until the police chief came to question him earlier this afternoon"

Kirsten had to give Chief Hall credit for following up like she said she would. "What did he tell the chief?"

"He was asleep when she came by." Mrs. Fairbanks shrugged. "She said she needed to talk to some other folks, but she'd stop at his room later this evening." She frowned. "Why are you so concerned?" Her attention shifted to Kaley. "Is something going on between you and my son I need to know about?"

"Well, I'm not sure—" Kaley started.

"Not something between them directly, Mrs. Fairbanks," Kirsten interjected. "But it's no secret at school Josh and Kaley like each other. While it's just a theory at this point, someone may not like the idea of a Normal and a witch dating."

Mrs. Fairbanks's cheeks glowed bright pink, and she cleared her throat. "I appreciate you girls dropping by." She produced a rather half-hearted smile. "I'll be sure to let Josh know you both stopped to check on him." She whirled and re-entered Josh's room.

What was that all about? Kaley asked.

I hate to say this, but I don't think you need to worry about dating Josh, Kirsten said.

"Wait! I didn't give him the box of chocolates," Kaley protested.

"You can give it to him as an apology present when he comes back to school." Kirsten tugged on her sister's arm. "Let's go talk to Tina before someone decides to bounce us from the hospital."

Kirsten trudged toward the elevator, a dejected Kaley by her side. Mrs. Fairbanks's bigotry cut her twin a lot deeper than she was willing to admit. Maybe they should both go to school somewhere out of state. Cut ties with Millersburg. She'd always believed the town was just dry and dull. Maybe the bigotry had always been alive on all sides her entire life, and she'd been too naïve to see it.

The instant she jabbed the button to go down to the first floor, the elevator dinged, and the doors opened to reveal Mr. Fairbanks holding two large cups from Jo's shop. From the delicious odor, both drinks were the pecan praline-flavored lattes Jo had let Kirsten develop. Josh definitely got his height and good looks from his dad, except Mr. Fairbanks had silver hair threaded through his dark locks like her own dad.

"Hi, Mr. Fairbanks," Kirsten said as he stepped out of the car.

He grinned. "Hey, girls. Is Josh awake? Did you get to talk to him?"

"No, he wasn't." Kaley made a good show of her usual cheerfulness. "We didn't want to disturb him." She held out the box of peanut butter cups. "I forgot to leave these for him. Would you please give them to him and tell him we hope he feels better?"

"Sure." He held both cups in one hand for a moment and tucked the box of candies beneath his armpit. "How did you like that necklace he gave you, Kaley?"

"Necklace?" she choked.

"Oh, crap." He winced. "I spoiled the surprised, didn't I?"

"It's okay." Kaley smiled. "It's nice he was thinking of me."

Kirsten sucked in a deep breath at her opportunity. "I saw it when he showed it to Donny. Do you know where Josh got that necklace? I'd like to find something that unique for our mom."

"I'm pretty sure he bought it at Nana's." He chuckled. "In fact, the new Safewide regional director asked him that very question. She was checking it out when he stopped by the office last week to show it to me."

"The new Safewide regional director?" Kirsten choked out. Her sister's shock washed over her, adding to the muddle her thoughts had become.

"Yeah, Cissy Martin's daughter Heather. She said her son was in your class."

"He is," Kaley said. "He was sitting with Donny and our parents when Josh got sick."

Mr. Fairbanks's expression shifted to a scowl. "Chief Hall was rather cagey about what happened to Josh. She said there was an explosive device found on my son. She claimed the leaking chemicals are what caused his internal bleeding."

"She doesn't think Josh is guilty if that's what you're worried about," Kirsten interjected.

"How would you know?" Mr. Fairbanks demanded.

Kirsten lowered her voice. "This can't go any farther than us."

"All right." He nodded.

"We think the real target was my sister."

Chapter 29

Kaley wanted to kick her twin in the shins, but not in front of Josh's dad. "Kirsten's exaggerating a bit. But Chief Hall is pretty sure the same person who set the bomb in the Painter Building is also the person planted the bomb on Josh."

"Josh said you got hurt pretty bad." Mr. Fairbanks's frown deepened.

"Mainly a concussion, which is why there are two of you, and my seeing eye twin drove me to the hospital." Kaley jabbed her thumb in her sister's direction.

As she spoke, the elevator opened again and deposited more visitors.

"We'll let you get back to Josh. We hope he's better soon." Kirsten tugged on Kaley's jacket to get her in the car.

"Thanks," Mr. Fairbanks murmured. He was still watching them with a slightly suspicious look when the door slid shut.

"You shouldn't have said anything," Kaley snapped.

"What was I supposed to do?" Kirsten said. "Couldn't you feel his worry? It was the same fear Dad had when you were in the ER the other night."

"But what if you tip off the real culprit?"

"That was my plan."

Kaley wanted to slap her twin's smug look off her face. "What in the Goddess's thousand names are you talking about?"

"If River's innocent, who else in town has access to fae magick?"

Kaley blinked. "You can't be serious. Ms. Martin was definitely worried about River last night."

"Because she screwed up whatever she's using to delay the magicks from interacting too soon."

They reached the main floor, and the doors opened. Kaley bit her tongue to keep from asking her sister any more questions in front of the Normals. But the more she thought about Kirsten's theory, the more it made sense. Heather Martin had more than enough motive to hate this town and the people in it. Furthermore, she couldn't imagine Mom and Dad tossing her or Kirsten out on their ear if they accidentally got pregnant.

And since River was practicing wards, healing, and small charms, all his mom had to do was ask for a good luck or protection spell, and she'd have her ammunition. Except the fae magick she used didn't come from River, so who was Heather's source?

Kaley followed her sister through the admin offices and back to the accounting department.

"Hey Jeannie!" Kirsten said brightly. "Is your boss available?"

Tina's administrative assistant peered over the tops of her bright pink reading glasses. Tina let her staff display their individuality much to the hospital board's chagrin, but the old fogies couldn't argue with her results.

"She's available, but I wouldn't go in there if I were you." Jeannie lowered her voice. "The police chief was here earlier. I think she questioned Tina about the two explosions in town." She smiled at Kirsten. "Though I heard the Lady Knights pulled off the win last night before everything went to heck in a handbasket."

"Thanks." Kirsten nodded.

"We'll take our chances with your boss," Kaley said. "This is kind of important."

Jeannie shrugged. "It's your funeral."

Kaley strode to Tina's closed office door and knocked.

"I said I didn't want to be disturbed!" Tina was rarely this irate. Chief Hall must have really gotten under the witch's skin.

Kaley twisted the knob and shoved the door open. "This is a coven matter."

Tina's scowl faded. "What are you girls doing here?"

"We need to talk," Kaley said.

Once Kaley and Kirsten spilled the incidents around the two explosions, Tina leaned back in her office chair and scrubbed her eyes. "You two aren't telling me anything Chief Hall didn't say during her visit. After Jimmy came by my place Wednesday night, I'd already called Nana and had her pull any jewelry she was selling on consignment for me. The loss of income is going to make a huge dent in my budget for Noah and Mila's wish lists for the holidays."

"Can you make some new pieces?" Kaley asked.

"I can, but November's my best month." Tina sighed. "I'll have to take everything Nana's pulled and wash them in salt water to remove the charms I put on them." Tina sighed and rested her elbows on her desk. "Neither the chief or Jimmy would tell me what was making my jewelry turn into bombs. Thanks for letting me know about the fae magick. I just can't imagine how or why either court would bring anything with their spells to Holmes County. Even the Accords list us as off limits to the fae."

"We have our suspicions," Kaley said. "However, we can't say anything right now. Chief Hall and Uncle Jimmy have recruited Kirsten for an internship in January, and they've got her working on this case a little early."

Tina's frown deepened. "Wouldn't that be a conflict of interest since you got hurt in the first bombing?"

"Under normal circumstances, it would," Kirsten replied. "But all the adult witches in town except you, Noah, and Mila are also relatives of ours, and they have regular jobs. Does Nana keep a record of who bought your pieces?"

Tina reached behind her desk, and a drawer squeaked. She produced her phone. "Both Nana and I already gave copies to the police and sheriff's departments. No reason I can't give one to you, too, since you're working with law enforcement." She looked up from her screen and eyed each sister. "But this is only for official use if Kirsten is interning with the police and sheriff's departments. You two got me?"

"Yes, ma'am." Kaley nodded along with her twin.

Kirsten's phone beeped and she checked the receipt before she stood. "Thanks for your help, Tina. We won't betray your trust."

She nodded. "Before I forget, can you babysit Monday, Tuesday, and Wednesday afternoon and evenings next week, Kaley? We have an auditor coming in and checking the books, and I'll be here late."

"No problem." Kaley waved her left hand nonchalantly. "And consider my fee a donation to the holiday present fund for the kids."

"I can't let you—" Tina started.

"This bomber has screwed up enough of our lives," Kirsten said fiercely. "Don't let them screw up your kids' holiday, too."

Tears glistened in Tina's eyes. "Thanks, girls. You two have gone above and beyond."

"See you Monday." Kaley waved.

The girls exited Tina's office and headed for the hospital's main entrance. Kaley could sense Kirsten's tension, but her sister wouldn't say anything, not even telepathically, until they were away from the mass of people entering and exiting the place.

Once they were ensconced in Mom's sedan, Kirsten handed Kaley her phone while she pushed the ignition button, shifted into reverse and backed out of their parking spot.

Kaley opened the document Tina had texted to her twin and scrolled through it. Air caught in her lungs. Josh Fairbanks had bought the necklace he planned to give her a week ago. Heather Martin bought three bracelets the following day, including a silver and obsidian one.

Swallowing hard, Kaley glanced at her sister. "This means River's mom is the bomber, and she's planning additional targets."

Chapter 30

Kirsten could feel her twin's nausea in her own stomach. "That's what I'm thinking."

"But who is she really after and why?"

Could Kaley really be that naïve? Kirsten sighed. No, her sister just saw the best in everyone. "K, not everyone has the wonderful high school life you do."

"Excuse me?" Kaley narrowed her eyes. "Amelia Ryder tried to deck me, I was pummeled in an explosion, my provisional crush is in the hospital, and I'm currently suspended from the cheerleading squad for skipping study hall of all things. That's just what's happened to me in the last month."

"You do know one of those things is not like the other three?" Kirsten teased.

"You're not funny, Miz Sarcasm," Kaley bit out.

"Think about Heather's motives," Kirsten said. "Who would she hate the most in town?" She could almost visualize the hamster running in her twin's brain to make the connections.

"Her mom for throwing her out after she got pregnant," Kaley said. "But why target the Painter Building and the high school?"

Kirsten tapped the left turn signal and braked at the red light for Jackson Street. "Look at the timing. Technically, the Painter Building was practice after Josh's necklace didn't go off right away." Kirsten ticked off her index finger.

Kaley frowned. "You think she screwed up on the mixed magick spell, which is why Josh got sick before it exploded."

Kirsten nodded. "Both incidents were to get the cops to think they had a serial bomber, and she counted on the evidence not making conventional sense. She didn't know about Julia's background or Chief Hall's taskforce." She ticked off her middle finger. "Finally, she'll take out her mom. My guess would be at the Hair and Now during the day while it's busy." She ticked off her ring finger.

A pickup truck behind them honked. Kirsten checked that the light was green and there was no oncoming traffic before she completed the turn.

"To tie in with what should have happened at the high school." Kaley nodded slowly. "Except you and Mom kept the magick bomb going off."

"No, it went off," Kirsten snarled. "We just managed to get it out of the building before it did."

"Unfortunately, she has two more bracelets Tina made." The worry in Kaley's voice scraped across Kirsten's nerves.

"But Chief Hall and Uncle Jimmy have cut off her source of witch magick in town," Kirsten said. "She's not going to have an easy method to get more once we tell Mom and Jo, and they contact the Brown Dog enforcers."

Kaley gasped, and Kirsten glanced at her sister whose eyes were wide.

"If she needed more, her easiest targets would be Noah and Mila," Kaley choked out.

The nausea in Kirsten gut grew worse. "But they can't do anything with their powers bound."

"But Ms. Martin won't know they can't." Ashy fear rolled off Kaley's psyche. "What if she threatened the kids to force Tina to give her more charmed objects?"

"Call Tina." Kirsten flipped the left turn signal and pulled into Millersburg Elementary. "Tell her were taking the kids to Miz Rose's."

"Why not our place or Jo's?" Kaley asked.

"That will be the first place Heather Martin will look for them." Kirsten did a U-turn in the parking lot and headed back toward Clay

Street. "And we've warded the heck out of Miz Rose's after Noah's dream form was harassing her. Also, call—"

"Miz Rose, Mom, and Dad. I will," Kaley assured her.

Kirsten tapped her fingers on the steering wheel as she waited for the red light at Clay to change. When the green arrow shone, it took all of Kirsten's willpower not to speed in the town limits. Tina's kids were only home for two hours between the school bus dropping them off and Tina getting home from work. Both kids were responsible under normal circumstances. They wouldn't let a stranger in the double-wide they called home.

But these weren't normal circumstances, and Goddess only knew what other fae tricks Heather Martin may have up her sleeves.

By the time Kirsten pulled into the Eislers' asphalt driveway, not only had Kaley called Tina, Miz Rose and their parents, she'd phoned Uncle Jimmy. He promised to alert the police department and issue a BOLO on Heather Martin.

When they reached the front door of the trailer, Mila yanked it open and glared at them. "What's going on? Mommy sounded scared on the phone."

Noah charged out of the hallway, carrying a black tote with a sugar skull pattern. "Our bags are ready."

"Why is Mommy sending us to Miz Rose's house?" Mila demanded.

Noah didn't say anything, but he obviously wanted to know the answer to his sister's question.

Kirsten eyed Kaley, who gave a subtle shrug and silently said, *Your choice.* The truth had always been Kirsten's preference, but she needed to be careful how she worded this for eight-year-old Mila.

"Someone's been using the charms your mom laid on the jewelry she makes to hurt people," Kirsten said. "Nana's taken everything off the shelves of her store, but our suspect has already bought several items."

"And the bad guy's already used two of the pieces to create bombs." Noah scowled. "That's what really happened to the Painter Building and at the high school last night, isn't it?"

"Yeah, it is," Kirsten admitted.

"But what does that have to do with us?" Mila blinked, her expression wide and innocent.

"It means Kirsten and Kaley are afraid the bad guy us will come after us to make more." Noah's eyes narrowed, daring them to lie in front of his sister.

"We would never!" Mila's anger flared, the emotion almost powerful enough to shred the binding spell that held her powers in check. "Even if we could!"

Kaley knelt in front of the girl. "We know you wouldn't, sweetie."

"They're worried the bad guy will threaten us to get Mom to cast spells they can use." Noah's chin jutted up at his words. Another challenge.

"That's exactly what we're worried about," Kirsten said. "Are you two ready to go?"

Noah dropped his attitude. "We can't get Agatha out from under Mom's bed." He held up his right arm to show the cat-in-flicted scratches.

"I'll get her." Kirsten tossed the car fob to Kaley. "Get everyone else and their luggage in the car. If you see anything suspicious—"

"I'll get the kids out of the line of fire, and call Uncle Jimmy. Witches' honor." Kaley held up her right three fingers.

Kirsten rolled her eyes. "That's the Girl Scout salute."

She strode down the hall and checked the utility room. Agatha's cat carrier wasn't in there. She entered Tina's bedroom. The overhead light was still on, and the carrier sat on top of the other witch's black comforter. Hissing came from beneath the bed.

Kirsten laid on the lint-covered burgundy carpet and peered

under the bed. Green eyes stared at her, the only indication of the cat's location. Agatha hissed even louder. She must be picking up on Noah and Mila's anxiety. Kirsten took a deep breath—

And explosively sneezed.

As much as she hated chores, maybe a thorough cleaning of the trailer would be a good Solstice present for Tina.

The noise did startle Agatha enough she no longer hissed. Kirsten concentrated and sent an image of protection and caring to the cat. It was a little more difficult to communicate to other witches' familiars, but Agatha meowed.

This time, Kirsten sent a different set of images, including Noah and Mila in seatbelts and Miz Rose's house. She must have gotten her point across to Agatha. The cat crept out from under the bed, leapt onto the comforter, and entered the cat carrier without any more fuss.

"Thank you, Agatha." Kirsten closed the door of the carrier and latched it.

The cat meowed and sent an image of her favorite treats.

Kirsten grinned before she mentally assured the cat she would adequately be rewarded for her cooperation.

Chapter 31

Kaley relinquished the driver seat to Kirsten once she deposited Agatha in her carrier plus her box of treats between Noah and Mila in the back seat. Her phone constantly beeped with a flurry of messages between all the adults.

River would be devastated if his mom was behind the bombings. While Heather may have some justifiable anger at her own mother, it didn't mean Miz Cissy deserved to die. Maybe it would be best to warn River. Kaley dashed off a text to him.

U at ur grandma's?"

She breathed a sigh of relief when he texted back immediately.

Yeah what's up?

Reason to believe she's next target. Is ur mom home from work yet?

No, been wrkng l8 every nite since we moved here. Y?

Double-check ur wards. Will explain when we get other potential targets 2 safety.

His answer was a thumbs up emoji.

You didn't tell River we suspected his mom, did you? Kirsten asked.

Give me a little credit, Kaley retorted.

"Mom says it's rude to talk telepathically in front of other people," Mila said.

"I, uh, forgot Agatha's litter box," Kirsten said.

"And I said we had an extra," Kaley added. "Sorry, Mila. We didn't mean to be rude. After we drop you off at Miz Rose's, I'll go to our house and grab it and some kitty litter."

"And some food, too?" Noah suggested.

Kaley giggled from her overwrought nerves. Nothing was going right this week. "I guess we're not that great in an emergency."

"Yes, you are," Mila proclaimed. "You figured out the blue ghost dog was really Noah. Maybe you're forgetting because you got your brains rattled the other night."

"I'm afraid to ask what my excuse is," Kirsten said dryly.

Kaley snorted. "Your big brain was so worried River would be the trouble-maker you're not paying attention to the real problems."

"Gee, thanks, sis," Kirsten grumbled.

Kaley's phone beeped again. "Jo says to take the alley behind Miz Rose's house and park in the old horse barn."

"That's because your car looks like crap," Noah said. "I wouldn't want you parked in front of my house either."

Kirsten's irritation at Noah's attitude grated against Kaley's nerves. She couldn't blame Noah. He would have preferred going to his dad's house. Maybe the kid had a point. A hunting rifle could do a lot of damage to both a fae and a Normal.

Mila piped up. "It's so the bad guy doesn't see their car. Everyone in town knows it was dinged along with the other folks' cars in the auto parts store parking lot when the Painter Building got blown to bits."

"Both of you need to cut out the bickering," Kaley said. "It's bad enough someone's using our own magick against us. We don't need to be fighting amongst ourselves, too."

"Yes, ma'am," the kids said in unison.

Agatha let out a very upset meow.

Kaley wasn't sure what was worse—Noah and Mila snapping at each other, the poor cat picking up on everyone's crazy emotions, or being called ma'am.

There's worse things they could have called you, Kirsten pointed out silently.

You're not helping, Kaley shot back.

Actually, nothing would until they caught whoever was causing trouble. And she feared if it were Heather Martin, it might sink whatever thing was budding between her and River.

Kaley breathed a little sigh of relief when she saw the barn doors were open and Jo waited inside for them. Her aunt's car was already parked in the barn. Kaley climbed out of Mom's car and said, "Any news?"

Jo shook her head. "Every witch is safe for now."

"I texted River to warn him that his grandmother's next on the list," Kaley admitted.

"You what?" Jo was obviously going to say more before she noticed Noah and Mila paid a little too much attention to their conversation. She smiled at the younger kids. "Why don't you two come inside the house? Rose made pumpkin cookies, and she has a gallon of cold cider waiting for you."

Agatha meowed pitifully from her carrier, which Kirsten handled along with her backpack. Leave it to her twin to be worried about homework in the middle of a crisis. Noah and Mila carried their overnight bags.

"She has milk for you, too, little one," Jo assured Tina's familiar before she closed the huge barn doors and led them out the people door.

Together, they trudged across Miz Rose's backyard. Every plant, even the mums, were brown while their roots slept through the winter. Kaley understood the cycle, but the dormant flora was rather depressing.

They entered Miz Rose's mudroom and hung up Noah and Mila's coats before they entered the kitchen. Kaley wasn't the only one surprised to see Officer Hatfield perched on one of Miz Rose's kitchen chairs, munching on a pumpkin cookie.

Except he wasn't wearing his uniform. Jeans, boots, and a green and blue flannel shirt were the outfit of the evening.

He swallowed his bite and smiled. "Hi, Kaley! Good to see you walking around."

Jo introduced him to Noah and Mila while Kirsten set down the cat carrier and released Agatha. She stalked around the kitchen, examining everything like she owned the place. Without being asked, Miz Rose set a bowl of milk on a rubber mat along with a dish of water.

"Noah. Mila. It's good to see you." Miz Rose beamed. "Why don't you two take your bags upstairs along with your mother's? Then wash up and get back here before Mark eats all of the cookies."

For the first time since puberty hit Noah, he didn't argue. "Yes, Miz Rose." He and Mila headed out of the kitchen and down the hallway to the main staircase.

Kirsten crossed her arms. "What are you doing here, Officer Hatfield?"

"Get your hackles down," he said softly. "The chief's worried. She agrees with your theory."

"Your mom's with the chief now at the Safewide office," Jo added. "Heather apparently left work early, claiming she had some moving errand to take care of."

"That can't be," Kaley protested. "River's at Miz Cissy's place guarding her because his mom's working late."

"Heather could have just as easily lied to him and Cissy as she did to her secretary," Officer Hatfield pointed out. "I'm staying here with you guys until a patrol or your mom finds her."

"Crap," Kaley muttered. "We need to run to our house for an extra litter box. We forgot to grab Agatha's."

"That's not a good idea," Officer Hatfield said.

"Neither is a poor cat pissing all over my house," Miz Rose snapped. Agatha finished her milk and rubbed herself around the elderly woman's ankles.

Jo sighed. "I'll take Kaley over to their place and gather what we need and come straight back here. Will that satisfy you, Mark?"

"I'll say you cast a spell on me if you get yourself into trouble, Jo. I'm not taking the fall for you." He smiled to ease the bite of his words before he reached into his pocket, pulled out his keys, and tossed them to Kaley. "Take my SUV. It's parked out on the street. Try not to bring it back as pockmarked as your mom's car."

"I'll do my best," Kaley said. "Ready, Jo?"

Her aunt ducked into the mud room and came out wearing her coat. "Let's make this fast. I don't like you being exposed with some nutcase running loose."

Kaley swallowed her reply, which would only make the situation worse. At least, Jo wasn't blaming River for the situation anymore.

Chapter 32

Fortunately, the Wilson house was dark when Kaley pulled into the driveway. The huge old maple shadowed most of that side of the house. If any Normal was watching, they couldn't make out who exited Mark Hatfield's SUV. Jo followed Kaley to the back door.

"Don't turn on the main lights," Jo ordered.

"Wasn't going to." Kaley strode over to the stove and flipped on the microwave light over the burners. "Would you grab the extra bag of food in the pantry?"

She went back out to the mudroom to retrieve Glinda's litterbox. Even though Mom's familiar had passed away three years ago, she still grieved. Kaley had tried dragging Mom to the animal shelter, but none of the cats there spoke to her. Maybe Mom needed a different animal for her new familiar. Like a dog or a ferret.

Kaley grabbed a plastic shopping bag from the recycle bin. After checking it for holes, she scooped kitty litter from the five gallon bucket into the bag and tied it. She carried both items into the kitchen where Jo stood at the sink, refreshing Teller and Penn's water bowls.

A loud meow demanded her attention. She picked up Penn and scratched under his chin.

"Don't worry. I wasn't going to forget to feed you." She set him back down.

Teller stalked out of the shadows beneath the kitchen table and meowed his inquiry to where his human was.

"Kirsten is helping Agatha guard Noah and Mila," Kaley said while she filled each cat's food bowl.

"Maybe we should take the boys with us," Jo said.

"They'll be okay here," Kaley assured her aunt.

"With a mad, magickal bomber on the loose?"

A loud knock on the front door interrupted whatever Kaley was about to say. "Oh, crap. With everything going on this afternoon, I forgot Hope and Donny were coming over for dinner tonight."

"That's not Donny on the porch," Jo murmured.

Kaley reached out and felt the familiar ethereal quality of fae magick. "It's River." She glared at Jo. "Something's wrong if he came here."

She ignored her aunt and strode into the living room and flipped on the room's lights and the porch light. She yanked the front door open, but River wasn't alone on the porch. And the woman with him definitely wasn't his grandmother.

"Hey, River." Kaley forced a smile. "Ms. Martin. I'd invite you in, but Aunt Jo and I were just about to leave, and no one else is home at the moment."

A mix of worry and fear flowed from River. His face was sickly beneath his tan despite the warm yellow glow from the porch light.

Heather Martin wore a pleasant expression, but it didn't quite reach her eyes. Her right hand was in her coat pocket. "Our business won't take long, Kaley."

Jo stepped close behind Kaley. "We were just taking some extra cat supplies to a friend. You're more than welcome to ride along, and we can talk."

"Sure," River said.

"Really? I thought you were having tacos with your friends tonight, Kaley, dear." Heather's words contained a chill that rose goosepimples on Kaley's skin. "A taco dinner my son was specifically excluded from."

"If River wasn't invited, the fault is mine and Rachel's, Heather," Jo said. "Not the kids. I apologize for the way we acted last night—"

"I don't think so, honey," Heather said. She pulled her hand out. It held a gun. "I wouldn't suggest any spells, ladies. It's loaded with bullets impregnated with fae magick."

"Mom!" River stared at her in horror. "What the f—"

"I'm doing this for your own good, sweetie," Heather said. She waved the gun. "Let's go inside."

"Mom, no." River stepped between Kaley and his mother.

"It's the only way to make sure your father pays for what he did to us."

"By punishing innocent women?" he exclaimed. "Besides, he's probably dead after the battle between the fae and the other supernaturals in the county years ago."

"Inside, sweetie." Heather smiled up at him. "Or I'll shoot your little girlfriend."

"C'mon, Kaley." Jo tugged on her coat. "Let's go into the living room." *We go along until help arrives*, Jo whispered in Kaley's mind.

"It's okay, River." She raised her hands. "We'll do as your mother says." She slowly turned and headed back into the house, expecting a bullet in her back at any minute.

Chapter 33

Kirsten?

She jumped at the unexpected telepathic contact, knocking over her glass of cider. *River?*

My mom's off her rocker. She's holding Kaley and your aunt at gunpoint inside your house.

"What's wrong?" Officer Hatfield demanded.

The only person not staring at Kirsten was Miz Rose who retrieved a roll of paper towels and was mopping up the mess Kirsten had made on her kitchen table.

"Kirsten?" Hatfield said again.

"She's talking to someone else telepathically," Noah informed the policeman.

"Be quiet. All of you." Kirsten held up a hand. *Where are you?*

Sitting next to Kaley on your living room couch, River said. *Mom's not listening to me. She thinks killing your family will turn all the supernaturals against the fae. Somehow, she has bullets infused with fae magick.* River filled her in on his mom calling him, claiming she had a flat tire. He felt desperate, which meant if Kirsten didn't figure something out and quick, he would do something stupid.

Kirsten blinked. "I gotta go. Call Chief Hall and Sheriff Birkheimer. Tell them we've got a hostage situation at our house—"

"I'm coming with you." Hatfield started to rise.

"No. Tell them it's Heather Martin." Kirsten jumped to her feet. "Don't let my mom go home. Heather wants to kill her and Aunt Jo in the hope of starting a war between the supernaturals." Kirsten turned and ran for Miz Rose's mudroom. She slung on her coat and yanked the car keys out of her pocket.

And nearly ran into Donny at the back door.

"Heather Martin is at your house with a gun," he said.

"I know."

He jogged along beside her as she ran for the barn. She should tell him to stay here, but his steady confidence was so damn reassuring.

"I'll drive," he said. "You keep talking to Kaley."

Kirsten turned the corner to see Donny's car parked in front of the barn doors. "It wasn't Kaley who contacted me. It was River."

"He's not helping his mom, is he?" Donny asked as they climbed into his ancient vehicle and buckled their seatbelts. He started the engine, threw the car into gear, and peeled down the alley.

"Definitely not," Kirsten said. "Somehow, she got a hold of bullets infused with fae magick."

"How is that even possible?" Donny glanced at her. "Fae can't touch steel any more than I can touch silver."

"I don't know." Kirsten gnawed on her lower lip as she listened to Heather through River. The guy was not joking. His mom was missing more than a few colors from her crayon box. "I need to warn Hope—"

"Don't worry. I already did when I spotted the Martins on your front porch. What's the plan?" Donny said. "You can't go in slinging spells."

"No." She gulped. "I'll be the distraction at the front door. You go in the back."

Donny parked two doors down from their house.

Jo, Kaley, is the back door open? Kirsten asked.

Yes, Jo answered.

"If I get busted for running around town naked, you are paying the fine," Donny growled from the backseat. He ducked out of the car.

Kirsten got a brief glimpse of his bare backside when he ducked down the alley. Between being an athlete and a were, he did have a very nice butt.

She took a deep breath and opened the car door. It was dang frickin' cold tonight. Last thing, the Wilson clan needed was to blow up their own home. She slung her backpack over her shoulder and trudged toward her house. She needed to act as normal as possible as she approached the porch.

Kirsten jogged up the steps and opened the front door. "Kaley, I'm home!" she yelled as she entered.

"We're in here!" Kaley yelled back. Hopefully, their shouting would cover any noise from Donny coming in the back door.

"Mom and Dad went to the grocery store . . ." Kirsten took in the scene, and her heart pounded. Was she selling this act?

"Hello, Kirsten." Heather Martin rose from the dining room chair she'd brought into the living room. She aimed the gun toward Kirsten. "I've been wanting to meet the little bitch who gave my son a rough time on his first day of school."

Kirsten raised her hands. "What's going on?"

"America wants a race war." Heather Martin smiled. "I'm merely providing one."

"Look, what went down between me and River was a misunderstanding on my part." Kirsten looked at him. "And I do owe you an apology, dude."

She turned back to Heather. "I get why you're angry, too. What River's dad did to you was wrong—"

"How would you know what he did to me?" she shrieked.

"—but our friend Hope is on her way here," Kirsten continued. "She's a Normal just like you. I'm asking you not to hurt her."

"Acceptable losses." Heather raised her gun.

She disappeared under a growling ball of red-tinged gray fur and shrieked as teeth and claws ripped delicate human skin. The gun discharged. Fae magick flared. The weapon landed on the carpet. Somehow, Kirsten and her family managed not to raise their wards and blow up the house. Teller bounded from in somewhere and batted the weapon over to Jo, who grabbed it.

River carefully knelt beside the bleeding, crying ball of torn clothing, shredded flesh, and shattered psyche that was his mother. Outside, sirens blared.

Donny padded over to Kirsten, a sad look in his gold eyes. He rubbed his head against her jeans-clad thigh, and she stroked his furry head.

Uniformed officers poured into the living room from all directions.

The adrenaline left Kirsten with a rush. Her legs started to shake, and she abruptly sat on the area rug. And all she could think was that she'd never get the tacos made tonight.

Chapter 34

Kaley watched as the paramedics rolled Ms. Martin out onto the porch. River's dejected expression tore at her emotions. Uncle Jimmy wouldn't let him ride to the ER with her. Chief Hall and Jimmy quickly separated everyone into different rooms of the Wilson house or, in a few cases, law enforcement vehicles in order to take everyone's statements.

Thankfully, Kaley ended up with Julia Wolford. The deputy made a point of taking Kaley out to her patrol SUV. She had the courtesy to let Kaley sit in the front seat. After the first round of questions, Julia went inside the house, but she left the engine running so there was some heat in the vehicle.

A little while later, Julia climbed back into her SUV and frowned at Kaley. "You said the gun discharged. Are you sure?"

Kaley nodded.

"Sweetie, the techs can't find the bullet."

"Wouldn't there be some kind of residue on the gun?" Kaley said. "It landed on the rug, and Teller swatted it over to Jo."

"The weapon will be tested, but it would help if we had the bullet as evidence," Julia said.

Kaley stared out the windshield and tried to remember what exactly happened. "Donny jumped on Ms. Martin and bit her wrist to get her to let go. The gun fired—"

She turned to Julia. "There was a flare of fae magick. I thought it was the spell on the bullet activating, but maybe it was River."

"What do you mean?"

"He's been operating on instinct for so long because he didn't have anyone to formally train him," Kaley mused. "Maybe he was trying to block the bullet and accidentally opened a portal to Otherwhere."

"Otherwhere?" Julie cocked her head. "You mean the place between places? That's how it was described to me."

Kaley nodded. "Yeah. Ask Donny if he smelled anything unusual besides ozone and gunpowder. It's the only other place the bullet could have gone."

In the end, enforcers from Brown Dog and Dare Covens came to Millersburg and assisted with the investigation. Not that Normal law enforcement needed help with Heather Martin. During her mad rants, she admitted she had set fire to the Crawford house back in Indianapolis after she asked Mr. Crawford to charm a couple of silver Celtic knots for hers and River's protection as well as the bullets for her handgun.

None of the enforcers could figure out how Heather triggered the mixed magicks. They claimed they would contact the St. James Coven for advice. They were able to confirm River had in fact sent the bullet to Otherwhere, even if it were totally by accident.

There was a hullabaloo among the supernaturals about what to do with such a powerful and untrained half-fae. Cissy Martin surprised everyone by insisting River would stay with her. Mr. Gryffudd offered to fly River out to Las Vegas for formal education, but Cissy said River couldn't go until the longer school holiday breaks and for summer vacation. She claimed he needed to know how to deal with Normals since he was half-Normal, and by gum, she was going to take care of her grandson.

Kaley rather suspected Miz Cissy felt guilty as heck about how she treated her own daughter. However, she didn't invade Miz Cissy's mind to find out for sure.

River was out of school for the entire following week. Kaley texted him a few times, offering to pick up his homework. On Friday, her anger flared when Mom suggested giving him some space.

Dad took Kaley out for a private dinner at the Millersburg Brewing Company on Saturday night, just the two of them.

"Sweetie," he started after the waiter took their drink and dinner orders. "I think your mom's right. River has had a lot thrown at him over the last few months. Moving to a new state and dealing with a new school. Losing a mentor. Meeting a grandmother he's never known. Dealing with his father's heritage is only the tip of the iceberg he's facing."

"I know, but Mom hates him just because he's part fae." Kaley threw up her hands.

"Actually—" Dad messed with the self-adhesive napkin ring. "This can't go beyond us. Not even Kirsten. Understand?"

Kaley nodded. Whatever Dad was hiding must be really bad if she couldn't talk to her twin about it.

"When the detectives and the enforcers finished analyzing everything, they realized if River hadn't accidentally opened the p-portal—" Dad squeezed his eyes shut.

She wanted to force him to say the words, and at the same time, she didn't want to know whatever he was about to tell her.

"The bullet would have hit you." He opened his eyes, and excess moisture shone in them. "And it most likely would have killed you. Mom and Jo lightened up about him quite a bit since this is the second time River saved your life. This isn't about your mother wanting you to stay away from him."

Kaley leaned against the back of the booth. The knowledge was almost too much. Nothing really bad had happened to her in her life before this. Not even getting suspended from the cheer squad for a week after she skipped study hall.

"D-do you think River doesn't want to be around me because of what his mom did?"

"I don't know, sweetie." Dad shot her a wry smile. "I hate to say this because you are the center of my world, but his lack of communication might not have anything to do with you."

The waiter dropped off their pops, and she waited until he was out of earshot before she added, "I guess I'm acting as conceited as Kirsten claims."

"I wouldn't put it that way." Dad unwrapped his straw and stuck it in his glass. "For being identical twins, you each have very different priorities in life. You want to help someone who you saw being treated unfairly. There's nothing wrong with that. You're a lot like your mom in that way. Whereas Kirsten and I need some space to deal with our feelings before we can talk about them. All you can do is be there when he's ready to talk."

"And you're saying River may be more like you than like me."

He nodded. "It doesn't mean any of us are wrong."

"Just different," she replied.

Dad nodded again.

"Thanks for helping me understand." She smiled at him.

"Not too shabby for a Normal, huh?"

They both laughed.

Later that night right after Kaley had crawled into bed and turned off her bedside lamp, her phone beeped. She picked it up and checked the text. It was from River.

> Sorry I haven't texted you back. Been at the hospital a lot. I was able to heal Josh, but not Mom. I don't know enough about mental illness. Mr. Gryffudd said it's nearly impossible for any healer. Anyway, I'll see you Monday at school.

Kaley thought about what Dad had said over dinner before she replied.

Kaley set the phone back on her nightstand and laid back down. Maybe Dad was wrong about River. Maybe he was more like her. It would suck if she had the ability to heal, only to discover she couldn't do a dang thing for her family.

At least River was talking to her again. She hoped he understood that family wasn't always the people related by blood. But in her case, she was rather glad her own blood treated each other like family.

Chapter 35

Wind blew around Kaley as she leaned against the brick wall of West Holmes High School and waited for River. She didn't bother using her abilities to block the breeze. The first bell rang as his beat-up Jeep pulled into the parking lot. Other students scurried past her and into the warmth of the building.

River, however, took his dear, sweet time. When he reached the doors, he stopped and stared at her.

"Are you okay?" he said at the same time she said, "Is your mom okay?"

They both chuckled.

"Let's get inside," she said. The cold and wind didn't bother either of them, but there was no sense getting a tardy slip from their trig teacher.

"I could heal her physical injuries," River murmured. She could barely hear him over the cacophony of students slamming lockers and rushing to class. "But I don't have the slightest clue about how to fix her mental problems."

"That's going to take some time," Kaley said.

"Tell your mom thanks for helping mine to get her into a good psychiatric hospital," he said.

"That was my aunt Jo." She smiled up at him. "Calling in some markers is her way of apologizing to you for making poor assumptions. How's staying at your grandmother's house?"

"It'll do for now." A rueful grin crossed his face. "I think she finally understands what really happened. Let's face it—" He scowled. "—what my sperm donor did to Mom was the equivalent of a magickal roofie and rape. Then Grandma added on to Mom's issues by kicking her out of their home for being pregnant with me."

Kaley couldn't blame River for the waves of anger flowing from him. The air started to mist around their tennies. She jabbed her elbow into his rib cage.

"I understand how you feel, but get a grip."

He looked down and muttered, "Sorry." One or two kids noticed the mist before it faded from around their feet.

"It happens to all of us." She smiled up at him.

"Um—"

Nerves assailed her. Was this it? Would he ask her out?

River licked his lips. "Uh, my grandmother, she, well, uh . . ." He raked his left hand through his hair making it more spikey than usual. "She said it was okay for you, Donny, Kirsten, and Hope to come over Saturday night. We could download a movie. Maybe get some more of that McKelvey's pizza you introduced me to?"

Kaley tried not to let her disappointment show on her face. "That sounds like a plan."

Joy radiated from him though his expression remained the same emo one as before. He leaned closer. "I think we need to take this slow. Give your mom and aunt a chance to get used to it."

"I promise I won't let Mom or Jo throw fireballs at you." She made an "X" over her heart.

"It's your dad I'm worried about." River made a face. "He gave me a very detailed explanation of how he castrates piglets and lambs."

Mortification and humor warred in her head. The humor won, and she burst out laughing. "I promise not to let that happen either."

They entered the homeroom just as the last bell rang.

Mrs. Thomas stepped back from the whiteboard. "Ms. Wilson, Mr. Martin, since you two like living dangerously, you'll be up at the board first after roll call and announcements."

Heat flooded Kaley's face. *Let's take this slow.* Mrs. Thomas and the rest of the class could think whatever they wanted.

Kaley, on the other hand, was looking forward to knowing River Martin much, *much* better.

Magick and Murder

Kirsten Wilson kept an eye on the protesters across the street from Aunt Jo's coffee shop as she served their only two customers. The huge double-paned picture windows didn't block the crowd's shouts. The auras around the Normals who marched were ugly smears of gray, their hatred marring the usual rainbow colors of their auras. They paraded up and down the block of East Jackson Street in front of the Holmes County courthouse. The Normal protesters shot even uglier looks at the coffee shop as they shouted their awful slogans.

She wished all of them were simply people from Cleveland or elsewhere, but she recognized more faces than she was comfortable with, including Hope Stillwell's mom. A shiver ran through Kirsten. She and Hope had been tight since first grade, and she'd been to the Stillwells for more birthdays and barbeques than she could count. To think that Mrs. Stillwell harbored such a secret dislike for Kirsten made her sick.

People in Millersburg may get into a snit fit if the neighbor's dog pooped in their lawn. Maybe the occasional DUI or domestic abuse situation. But nothing so bigoted as marching in hatred because someone was different.

And she knew the crowd felt that hatred marrow-deep. Why else would they be marching on such a cold day the week of Thanksgiving?

None of this made sense. Heck, Jo's status as a witch had been an open secret in the area, long before the Rainier Outing revealed the existence of the supernatural races eleven years ago. The ladies in town often consulted her about their problems. A lot of farmers stopped in for a hot breakfast and even hotter coffee with a side helping of weather predictions. But with the current lawsuits questioning the supernaturals' status as United States citizens, some nasty elements in Normal society decided integration was something to be avoided at all costs.

An occasional dead leaf drifted down the street on the wind, a reminder the earth was settling in for its long winter sleep. But it was an unusually bright, sunny day for Ohio despite the steady, cold breeze.

The brilliant blue sky silhouetted the historic three-story stone courthouse. However, its imposing features didn't deter the protesters. Neither did the couple of police officers watching them to make sure they didn't get out of hand. A couple of the idiots had tried to annoy people heading into the courthouse, both Amish and English alike. But after one warning from the police, Warren Simon, the leader of Humanity Now, reined in his followers.

Kirsten nibbled on her lower lip. Why did anyone follow a man like that? There was nothing really imposing about him. He was average height and average build for a Normal in his forties. His sandy brown hair was thinning on top. His round black spectacles gave him an owlish expression. Standard khaki slacks and a navy jacket over his white shirt made him look like every other dad at the local basketball games. Scuffed dark brown loafers completed his dad ensemble. If he wasn't one of the top anti-supernatural leaders in the country, she would have mistaken him for an accountant.

Mary Levy joined Kirsten at the window. The ties of her prayer cap dangled over her shoulders, as startling white against her navy blue dress as her bleached apron. She'd given up on cleaning the tables, not that they really needed it. Her bucket of lemony sanitizer competed with the rich aroma of fresh ground beans. Beans that would go to waste. None of their usual weekday regulars were coming in. Not today. Not with the mob across the street.

"No good will come of this many angry English in town." Mary shook her head.

Even though Mary was a month younger than Kirsten, the Amish considered her an adult. Sometimes, Kirsten was envious of Mary's status in her religious community. Other times, not so much. Kirsten had been friends with Mary long before she met Hope, but the Levys never so much as commented on the Wilson family's differences from other English. Maybe because Mary's great-great-aunt had been a vampire.

The reporter from Cleveland's *The Plain Dealer* rose from his table. He'd come in for a sandwich and attempted to chat up Aunt Jo. She could be incredibly charming when she wanted to be, but she delivered only stiff politeness to him. The rest of the staff had followed her lead, maybe with a little less stiffness.

"Thank you, ladies." He nodded to Kirsten and Mary.

"Have a good day," Kirsten automatically replied with a smile.

He exited the café to a series of boos from the crowd that drowned out the ringing of the bell on the door. That left Rose Gleason, Jo's closest friend in town. The elderly, retired legal secretary sat in her usual seat in the front right corner of the café, sipping her cinnamon latte, and also watching the protesters across the street.

Jo joined Kirsten and Mary at the left window, her attention on the crowd as well. "Let's clean up and close up shop, ladies. We're not going to get much more business today."

"Isn't that giving in to these jerks?" Kirsten stared at her great-aunt. It wasn't like Jo to act intimidated by anyone.

You can protect yourself, Jo said silently. *Hell, even Rose can swing her cane like a pro polo player. But Mary won't defend herself if that crowd gets physical, and I don't want to see her hurt.*

She had a point.

Kirsten turned to Mary. "Let me give you a ride home."

For once, Mary didn't argue about being in a car. She merely nodded before she grabbed her bucket and continued wiping down the tables.

Twenty minutes later, everything had been swept, cleaned, and put away.

"Rose, I'll drop you off at your place," Jo said as the three of them put on their jackets. Mary placed her black bonnet on her head and wrapped her black shawl around her torso.

"I walked up here by myself," the seventy-year-old Normal snapped. "I can walk home." Rose strolled the four blocks from her old Victorian to the coffee shop every day there wasn't rain, snow, or ice.

"Miz Rose," Mary said gently. "Not even I'm foolish enough to walk home with those people across the street. There's no sense courting trouble when it's avoidable."

Rose glared at the Amish girl overtop the bright orange rims of her spectacles. "Maybe a good whack over their heads would knock some sense into those idiots."

"That's assault," Jo said. "And you know those assholes will press charges."

Rose's eyes narrowed behind her glasses. "What're you going to do? Hex me if I don't obey you?"

"Maybe I will, you old fart," Jo growled. Even though they were born the same year, Jo aged more slowly being a witch, which meant she could have passed for Kaley's mom. Even her older sister.

Or maybe Rose's granddaughter.

Kaley leaned close to Mary and said not so quietly, "Is this what we're going to be like in fifty years?"

"Probably." Mary giggled. "But I will not be wearing such color-ful eyewear—"

Glass exploded into the café from the left picture window.

Acknowledgements

Once upon a time, an agent berated me for writing about places I'd never been. So, I wrote about a place I used to know. Any mistakes may be deliberate in order to save the citizens of Millersburg, Ohio, from fallout, or they may be part of my faulty memory. So, please don't make assumptions about anything in this series.

The first version of this book was originally written during the first two months of the COVID-19 pandemic of 2020. My planned research trip died on the vine because of the lockdowns, but thank goodness for the internet!

My writing changed over that period as well. It became as dark and depressed as most of us felt during the lack of social connection and lingering winter. So, I pulled all three of the Millersburg Magick Mysteries. It wasn't my best work, and despite promising myself I'd never pull a George Lucas, it had to be done.

The summer of 2022, I managed to travel back to Millersburg for a real visit, and I dragged DH with me because he was stressed over the death of his father. A few things in Millersburg have changed, like the rejuvenation of downtown. Other things, not so much. The Amish buggies rolling through town alongside the logging trucks enthralled DH to no end. Immersing myself back in the town helped get my mind back into the right attitude to write these books properly.

Additionally, I owe a great deal of gratitude to JW Manus and Valerie Lennox for making my books look professional and awesome. Thank you so much, ladies!

And many hugs to my Darling Husband and my cuddle puppy Princess Bella for keeping me sane over the last five years between the cancer and the pandemic.

About the Author

Suzan Harden transitioned from writing information technology manuals for companies and legal articles for a law enforcement magazine to her first love, fantasy and science fiction in all their forms. She's the author of the Bloodlines, the 888-555-HERO, and the Justice series.